Threesomes Cum

Threesomes Cum

Hotwife has erotica FMF & MFM sex.
A threesome menage and more...

Samantha Writner

Passionate Books for Passionate People

PO Box 51911
Ft Myers, FL 33994
www.BlackWidowPublishing.com

Black
Widow
Books

Threesomes Cum
Hotwife has erotica FMF & MFM sex.
A threesome menage and more...

Black Widow Books may be ordered through booksellers or by contacting:

Black Widow Publishing, LLC
PO Box 51911
Fort Myers, FL 33994
www.BlackWidowPublishing.com
(904) BWP-8469 (904-297-8469)

Print ISBN: 978-0-9862559-2-2
Digital ISBN: 978-0-9862559-3-9

Printed in the United States of America

Editor: Susan Allen
Cover design & book design: Jennifer FitzGerald - www.MotherSpider.com
Illustrator: Ashley St. Lawrence

Any people depicted in stock imagery are models, and such images are being used for illustrative purposes only. Cover image copyright: Profile Pawelsierakowski at 123RF

WARNING: Due to the sexual content within this book it is not suitable for those under 18. This book contains adult themes which some readers may find objectionable and/or offensive, including graphic depictions of sexual intercourse. Please do not read if you find the above subject matter to be offensive. We support those under 18 experiencing life slowly and ask that you wait until you have lived what is considered 'normal' for a while first, before reading literary works such as these.

Acknowledge

All the great people who work with and for Black Widow Publishing. If it weren't for you I never would have ventured this journey.

Susan Allen, my editor. You are a pleasure to work with. It was a tough time seeing my words reworked.

Jennifer FitzGerald, my book designer. Wow is all I can say. It is beautiful.

Ashley St. Lawrence, your art has given a whole new aspect to my writing. I Love It!

Table of Contents

Prologue

Sitting naked in front of my mirror, I cup my breasts for a moment and then began brushing out my long dark curls. I secured my hair into a more professional look for work as I reminisced about the first girl I ever kissed.

My lips full with glossy shine, purse as I think about that kiss. What a thrill it had been, I had loved kissing her. I dared not tell anyone who worked for me, but at the time, I wanted to tell the world that I loved her. My husband would have been a bit taken aback if he had known I would have gladly left him for a woman, especially since he was the reason I had kissed her in the first place.

As a woman, it has always been more difficult to deal with what society deems acceptable, in and out of the work place. I could have been misconstrued as a lesbian, which I don't feel I am or was. It was ten years ago now. I had been in Japan on a contract job with my team. God, she was so beautiful. She had soft pale skin with a light spray of delicate freckles all over. Her hair was a shoulder length mass of soft, silky curls, the color of Texas clay. It was amazing being with her, yet I also enjoyed men to the fullest as well.

I love men in fact. How could I not. I owned a high-tech, engineering company, in an industry that was dominated by men. Almost every employee I ever hired was a man. Everyone who worked for me knew I was married…to a man. Being intimate with a woman… That would have thrown a new wrench into my already complicated world. I was afraid I might lose face with the guys on the job, that they might have thought less of me, less of a woman, less of a boss, less of *their* boss.

My working relationship with my crew was of the utmost importance, it was vital to our safety. If we slipped up, someone could have gotten seriously hurt. I assumed that this was what it might have felt like to be a child with a lot of siblings…hiding something from them I mean. I remember I wanted to tell them all, they were my only family, other than my husband of course, and I wanted to share my joy with them. I wanted them to see that I was with her, and that we were a happy couple.

Chapter 1

The year was 2002. We were a specialized team of experts. At that time, there existed about a dozen pieces of machinery in the world that only my team, and one other, were qualified to maintain. When I graduated back in 2000, I was lucky, I had an 'in'. My uncle had worked on these machines and I had been drilling him for information on the subject since before I got out of high school. He took me under his wing and taught me the business from the ground up. As soon as I was qualified, I applied my skills to gathering a team of experts ready to replace my uncle's team when he retired.

He had been talking about his retirement since I was young. He had his entire life planned out to the exact day. People even joked that he probably had an entry for his own death in his planner as well. I often watched his face when people would make the joke. A tiny twist of the side of his mouth led me to believe they were correct in that assumption. I guess that all of my planning reminded him that I was just as motivated and detail oriented as he had been.

One day, he finally realized why I was always so interested in what he did, I came to him with a full business plan, and a complete team already organized and ready to take over. He was so impressed, but he stuck around another year after his retirement specifically to coach me on anything I needed. I was shocked by that. I hadn't known until that point, that he was adaptable. I recalculated my own life accordingly. He was truly my mentor and idol.

My uncle showed me all the business tactics I would need to make the most money possible. The business made a serious boatload of money, especially when we would go 'out' on a contract. More so than when we were home making repairs.

A contract for us meant a machine was broken and the owners needed us to come fix it.

They didn't actually break per-se, they just got out of alignment. When we were home, we were making repairs to parts that often needed replacing. We also built new machines on occasion. Luckily, the business was so lucrative we never missed a payroll date, or paying our debts, even when we weren't actually working for any particular client. We always had plenty of money in the bank. It was a great gig.

One of the best perks of my job was that these machines were scattered all over the world, which meant I got to travel and work in some amazing locations. This particular contract in Japan would take us about three months. That was pretty standard for a re-alignment job.

My husband, Matthew, was not very happy about this, since we had not even made it to our first anniversary at that time. He really didn't even know what my job was. It was just so complicated, I didn't like trying to explain it to anyone unless I felt they had the education and intellect of a master's degree in engineering, or something equivalent, and Matthew definitely did not have either of those.

I'm not sure what I saw in him, other than his sense of humor. He was funny. I'll give him that. That was a big deal for me. My job was so highly technical that I always tended to gravitate toward people who were totally not... technical that is. Whenever I was off the clock, I wanted to be as far away from my work as possible. Humor and adventure was where I found my escape. I think if I had tried to explain my job to Matthew he would have been lost by the second sentence.

Matthew and I met at a party two years prior, just after I finished college. We hit it off right away. He joked about everything, and our witty banter was so natural. It just felt like the breath of fresh air I needed in my life. We dated for a while before we became exclusive and moved in together. We had a habit of partying hard then going home to have crazy good sex. I'm sure the sex was why Matthew fell for me. Not many women are as outgoing and open as I am in bed. I learned when I was young, that if you didn't ask for what you wanted, you wouldn't get it. I applied that lesson to all aspects of my life, including the bedroom. It drove him crazy when I would 'talk all dirty' as he called it. As I saw it, I was just telling him what to do so I would enjoy it too.

I liked the fact that he was never judgmental about the things I would do or say. I had had guys in the past that made me feel bad when I would use what they called 'crude or foul' words. I suppose they thought only men could say things like pussy or cock. It wasn't 'lady-like' enough for them. So, when Matthew came along with his jovial self, and absolutely loved my bedroom speak, encouraged it even, we were a hit.

In retrospect, I should have talked to him a bit more openly about my business. It would not have come as such a surprise the first time I 'went away.'

He knew my job was complex, and that was why we never talked about it. Matthew wasn't stupid. He had a different kind of smarts. He was more into being a good salesman. He liked talking to people. If it didn't involve socializing, and winning someone over to his way of thinking, his brain would freeze. Seriously! I had seen his face freeze and his eyes glaze over. It happened whenever I said anything about what I did for a living.

My business plan and team were well underway when Matthew and I met. It took me almost another year to gather the rest of my team and present my business plan to my Uncle, who was on board right away, and allowed me to take over the business almost immediately. I have always loved to travel, so when this business opportunity was finally a go, it was like a match made in heaven for me. I was able to utilize my crazy brainiac skills in a business which took me on lots of exotic vacations. There was only one drawback in my opinion, and that was that I didn't get to travel all the time. That is what I had always wanted to do.

I had actually gone on three 'away' contracts while Matthew and I were dating, but my team and I spent most of our time at home base study-ing, fixing parts, and building new machines for prospective clients. The travel assignments hap-pened only two or three times a year, which is most likely why Matthew didn't realize I would be gone for so long, and so soon after our wed-ding. He knew I would have to be away on work assignments occasionally. I think he actually thought I might give up going on contracts after we were wed.

I had a bit of a dry spell with away con-tracts which happened soon after we first moved in together. I'm sure he thought that was how the job would be, and that the three previous trips were a fluke, or a thing of the past. Then he popped the question and we got hitched. We had no way of knowing an away contract would coming so soon after our wedding, or that it would be for a job on the other side of the planet.

Matthew had been hinting that perhaps I should give up this 'silly' job, even before we tied the knot. It was not something I was willing to even consider, although I guess you could say that I sort of went along with him, just to make him feel more at ease with the situation. I didn't like arguing, and he didn't like talking about it. He continually tried to change the subject to a topic he did like talking about, a subject I wasn't too fond of; threesomes. That was his go to idea, it seemed, for every situation.

I had never really given much thought to being with a woman before Matthew brought it up. In fact, when he did bring it up, and I did think about it, I wanted to shove it out of my mind. It didn't seem to get shoved far enough though. He never got tired of asking me again and again. I know he was trying to nudge me into a 'yes'. He was hoping I would give in and give him 'every man's fantasy', the elusive three-some. Again, in order to not cause an argument, I would hint at considering it, and then once he was finished with his diatribe about how I would enjoy it too, I would put the thought away. I couldn't understand why he wanted... no, almost needed, another woman. After all, he had just won the hand of this one so recently. I remember thinking to myself: Was it a primal urge that drove a man to be so preoccupied with the idea of sowing his seed? Or was it just *my* husband?

Fast forward a few months and I was half-way around the world in Japan. Here's where the story gets interesting.

Matthew and I talked on the phone every night for just five minutes. We decided it would be better for our budget not to spend fifty dollars or more each day on phone calls. I was rather surprised that given the limit of a mere five minutes, his persistent pushing toward the threesome did not ease up. You would have thought we had better things to talk about in our tiny window of opportunity. I had been on the job site for only two weeks when during one of our evening phone calls, he asked if I would give him a 'present' when I came home. He was very clear what that present should be.

Ok, I thought, I'll play along for a bit, see if we can have some intimacy on the phone. Perhaps this is what he needs to be intimate and if I can give him a little of what he wants, perhaps he could see the light and start to give me what I want, passion and romance.

I asked, "And what would you like this present to look like?"

A short inhale from his end, and a bit more silence than what I expected followed before he answered. I must have thrown something into the mix that he actually had not expected. Perhaps I was wrong about him truly wanting this. Perhaps it's only the fantasy that he wants, not the reality.

Finally, he was able to expand upon his fantasy, "Well…ahhhh…I guess I hadn't really thought about it that far. If she looks like you that would work for me."

"What if I don't want a good looking girl?

If she is too good looking, what's to keep you staying with me?"

"Well, I don't want to do some dog. I have tastes, and if she isn't my type then I probably couldn't get it up for her anyway. I wouldn't actually enjoy it then, so what's the point?"

I could see his point there. It wouldn't really be a fantasy if both girls were not at least close to his liking. I conceded, "Ok, I get you. Do I get to pick her or you?"

"I think I should pick her." he said quickly.

I didn't like that idea at all. It just didn't seem right. I expressed my thoughts, "I don't think it will work well that way. I can see myself getting jealous if you choose who it will be."

He was quick to correct the situation. I could hear adolescent glee in his voice, the kind a kid gets when he knows he is about to get the present he has been waiting for all year. "Oh, no no no. That's fine then. You can pick her, although I have to be able to override if she doesn't do it for me."

That brought up another question of mine, "How exactly do we obtain this 'present'? We can't exactly go to one of our friend's parties and pick someone up that we know. It needs to be someone who is not in our circle of friends. I don't want anyone looking at me funny or whispering behind our backs."

"Yeah I know, that's fine, even though I

would have loved to have tried to get Stephanie as our third. She is so hot, don't you think?"

That was his not so subtle way of trying to get me to believe I would enjoy this so called 'present' as much as he would. I admit, I can admire a good looking woman, although I guess she must be pretty amazing for me to take notice. I didn't really feel it was natural for a woman to be checking out another woman. I'm supposed to be checking out men, right?

I replied, perhaps with a bit too much sarcasm, "Sure she is, but she's off the list." It didn't faze him. He continued on with giddy anticipation.

"Yes, whatever you say babe. I guess we would have to go to a bar or something to find her." I could almost picture him bouncing in his seat with enthusiasm.

I controlled the urge to roll my eyes even though he couldn't see me through the phone. "What bar? So, like what? Are we supposed to just walk down to our local tavern and pick up some hot chick and say, 'Hey babe, do you want to fuck us?' I'm not so sure that will work either."

"Wow babe, I had no idea you had put this much thought into it. I'm so glad you are on board with this, it's gonna be great. Once we get all the kinks worked out of the plan, of course."

"Sure babe, anything for you. Hey, I've gotta run. My five minutes is up. You think about all the 'kinks' and we can talk about it more tomorrow. Love ya."

As usual he groaned loudly at my announcement. He did this every time. It made me feel as if I had done something wrong. He hated that we only had five minutes, but that measly five minutes cost me a hefty penny. It would quickly eat up all the extra money I made on away contracts if we went beyond that. Why did he have to keep doing that? I hated it when he tried to make me feel guilty about being responsible with our money.

"Okay," he said with disconcertedness. "I will look into how we can locate a 'present'. You keep thinking too though. I want you involved every step of the way."

"Well thanks. I appreciate that you want me to be involved in getting you laid by another woman." I was not very happy with how excited he was being with all of this, the jealousy was creeping in. "Talk tomorrow. Bye."

"Bye."

I hung up, then stood up from the same private phone booth I used every night for our conversations across the ocean. We didn't have phones in the apartments we were staying in because we were on short term leases. Plus, I didn't want Ashley (my roommate) to hear my conversations, especially that one. I would not have been able to be professional with my team if they knew what was going on with my spouse.

After my call home was my favorite time of the day. At that late hour not as many people roamed the streets. I slowly walked past the closed stores, and enjoyed the night air and all the lights.

The Japanese loved their neon. Neon signs were everywhere. Every square inch was covered by some sort of advertisement that glowed, or flashed, or made music. Gigantic TVs played continual loops of advertisements in between music videos. It was like New York City escalated to a new level. Times Square on steroids. They loved to write in English too, although the grammar was all wrong.

Japan had a kind of modern beat intermingled with traditional. The oriental peaks of long ago castles were put on modern high-rise towers. American fast-food joints stood right next door to sushi houses. (Americans would cringe to see the authentic fare served there.)

The air was crisp, cleaner than New York. Few residents used cars there, so the environment seemed better. Maybe it was just how I felt about it.

Early December would not bring snow to this region, although it would be extremely cold. I welcomed the vending machine at the end of the street that delivered a steaming can of hot chocolate with a pop-top. I would keep it in my pocket, warming my right hand through my gloves, then switch to the other side. Back and forth, the can and my path, until the heat of my hands was greater than the can. When it was at last cool enough to drink, it was perfect. After such a long walk, my busy mind would finally be ready for sleep. I would sip my drink, the warmth carrying down into my stomach and the sugar revving up my engines.

When I arrived back at the apartment, I saw that Ashley was attempting to watch TV. My team, at that time, was made up of four guys and one girl beside myself, Ashley. We girls had an apartment together, and the guys had another.

Ashley and I watched TV pretty much as a joke. We got a laugh out of it, since neither of us spoke any Japanese, at least not at first. It was slowly coming to me. By the time we were ready to leave, I had a pretty firm grasp on it. I was always a very quick study of languages, besides, immersion into a society creates necessity.

"How's the show?" I asked.

She looked up to me from her cross legged position on the floor and smiled. "Oh, hey Terry. About the same as the last one. No idea what is going on. They have great clothes though."

She giggled, and my vibe started to shift. Even with my luxuriant walk, the phone call hung over me that night. She had a way of bringing me out of my moods, through the girlish nature that was Ashley. She was good at that. I could never stay in whatever funk I had landed in when I was around her. Finding someone with her qualifications, that just happened to also have a fun nature had been amazing. The guys were not quite so funny. They were all amazing brainiacs just like Ashley, but they definitely didn't go as far with the humor bug. Sam would make the occasional joke, but they were mainly about machines. (Not that it was bad to joke about machines in our line of work.) Everyone loved Ashley.

Laughter came from the TV, followed by two young girls heatedly talking to each other with waving arms. I removed my shoes and coat at the door and deposited the now empty hand warming cocoa can into the trash. I joined her on our floor, listening to the jumble of language that was foreign to our ears. The Japanese do not believe in the use of chairs, and our apartment was furnished in a traditional Japanese style.

We had one square table, that when we arrived sat in the middle of our small abode. There was enough room on all sides to have people sitting and still be able to walk around. Since it was just the two of us, and we didn't expect any company during our stay, we had shifted the table to a corner, just far enough that a person could sit between the wall and the table. This allowed us to prop the pillows against a wall, and create a pseudo chair for our American comfort. There were four soft pillows, one for each expected sitter at the table so we claimed two apiece.

The TV sat in the corner on a short pedestal so the screen was at eye level when you were seated. A soft bamboo mat was used on the floor. That was the custom for every floor in Japan. It stayed clean due to our employment of tradition; the removing of our shoes at the door. I truly enjoyed being barefoot anyway, I always liked my shoes off. I had decided to carry this tradition to my home, when I returned to the States.

The smell of cooked rice was in the air. Like most residences in Japan, we had a rice cooker that steamed away all day. As soon as the contents were emptied, it was promptly washed and the process would begin again. Measuring the rice, rinsing thoroughly until the water ran clear, adding to the cooker, filling with water to the line, closing the lid, and pushing the green light. Once the rice was finished the cooker would automatically switch to 'keep warm' mode. At least that's what I believed it said. The idea of actually learning to read Japanese seemed even out of my realm of intelligence.

Rather than laughing with Ashley at the comical, non-understanding of our entertainment, I must have let out an unconscious sigh as I sat down. She took notice that something was wrong.

"Was it not a good phone call today?" She inquired gently. She pointed the remote at the TV and the volume of the boink boink rhythm, that concluded the show, began to ebb away.

I shrugged my shoulders. "It was okay, I guess. He is having a hard time with me being gone so soon after our wedding. I told him my job would have me going away on long contracts occasionally. I've just never been on one since we've been exclusive. He'll have to get used to it I guess."

"That must be rough. It's hard to have make-up sex when you're five thousand miles away from each other." She winked and smiled, lightening the mood even more.

"He is quite actively planning our sexual escapades for my return."

Laughter barked out loud and it ran into her next word. "What?"

I tensed up. "Oh, nothing." Crap! I had never spoken on such a personal nature in her company. It was unlike me. That may have been what made her laugh so abruptly.

"Really?" She looked at me as if she were looking over librarian spectacles, then she got up and went to the kitchen. I heard glass clinking as she removed the sake bottle from the cupboard, and I heard what must have been the two small ceramic sake shot glasses. "This conversation calls for a drink, if I ever heard one," she said as she returned to her pillows, elegantly crossing her legs on the way down, to arrive Indian style at the bottom.

Hoping the conversation could be shifted away from my situation somehow, I accepted my first glass of sake gladly. As was tradition, we both raised our glasses, and together said, "Kanpai!" The shot went down cold liquid, turning to fire on the way.

The second night, after we arrived in Japan, the owner of our current contract had taken the entire team out to dinner. Sushi. An experience I will never forget. In America, Sushi is a loosely used word, and what one eats in America as sushi, does not compare to the true experience in the Orient.

Maju Son spoke fairly good English, as most Japanese learn from a very young age and for many years, something I wish we had the luxury of in our country. He taught us all of the customs that we should be aware of, and most especially taught the team the properness of sake. By the time we were stumbling home, after many bottles of sake had been passed, it was well ingrained into our bodies and minds. I digress.

I didn't take the time to contemplate more about what might transpire when I took that first shot though. The custom, with any group in Japan is, once you have opened a bottle of sake together, so must you all finish it together. Ashley immediately poured our second shots, and the ritual continued. I was definitely warm now, and I knew happy times were about to take over the emotional dumping ground in my mind.

"So!" Ashley began, seeming even more chipper than five minutes ago, as she poured the next round. "What has Matthew got planned for your return?"

I looked down at the cup I held in my lap, and wondered why I had brought this subject up. I didn't want anyone knowing that my brand new marriage could be on shaky ground, already. That my husband was already wanting, and was actively looking for another woman. How would Ashley respect me, or take orders from me, as her boss once she knew? I couldn't tell her. I shouldn't tell her. Yet, at this point in the conversation, with me about to partake of a third round of sake, I had no idea how I was going to get away from it.

"Kanpai my friend!" Ashley coaxed. "Never fear. Everything you are about to say will not only never leave this circle of trust, it will also be completely out of my mind by the time I have to call you 'boss' again tomorrow."

Was she reading my mind? I smiled, finally raising my glass to meet hers. It was still hanging in the air waiting for the tradition to be met. I swallowed hard.

"Have you ever kissed a woman?" I asked softly as I lowered my glass to the table. I couldn't believe I had just uttered those words.

Ashley's eyes widened just a hint, and with a smile she said, "Whoa! So he wants the elusive threesome already, huh?"

I was shocked. I guess it really was something that all men wanted. She knew the situation with just that one question.

My mouth literally dropped open, then I promptly shut it out of respect for the next question I needed to ask. Delicately, I queried, "Does that mean you have?"

"I have had three men who each asked me to have a ménage e trois, so I do happen to know a little bit about that question. I asked it myself once. I think it is the first question that all women ask another woman, after their significant other has brought up the threesome idea. Obviously, *you* have never kissed a woman."

"NO! Of course not!" I must have been blushing. My face felt hot. I wished I could take back all the words, the questions. I wished I could even put the sake back into the cupboard.

"Don't get all defensive on me. I don't think it's a bad thing. I believe we are sexual creatures, and to deny a sexual urge, with whatever sex the other person is, puts undue stress upon yourself, and others."

"So you *have* kissed a woman?"

"Yes." She paused, perhaps to let it sink in, it needed to.

Here I was, all concerned that she would think less of me, and she had kissed a woman, and didn't think anything of it. In fact, she thought it was natural. Ritual went right out the window, and I shot down my next drink, leaving her behind with a full glass.

She didn't allow it to phase her though, she simply followed suit, drank hers then filled our glasses again.

Hesitantly, I went in for more information. "So...did you like it?"

She snickered gently and smiled sweetly to verify her feelings, "What's not to like? Women are softer, they smell good, they're more attuned to what a woman wants, and they are prettier... Yes, I would say I liked it. We lived together for two years. I was, was people would call, a lesbian for a time."

"Oh! Wow! I didn't know." I stuttered over my words and looked away, searching for a way to get out of this conversation. Instead, I chased the awkwardness with another shot of sake.

"I don't know what you would call me now. I date men, usually. She was unusual, even for me. I like to look at women. I think they are so beautiful. Like you."

"What? You have been looking at me...like ...*that*?" I didn't know what to think at that point.

I was not sure if I should be offended that she had been ogling me, like a man would, or if I should take it as a compliment. She did say I was beautiful. Come to think of it, she was an amazingly beautiful woman herself.

I couldn't believe I had just done that! I ogled her!

I wondered if she would kiss me.

Oh my God! I was doing it again! I was acting like a man!

Ashley put her hand on my leg which made me twitch slightly. "It's ok. I think we look at anyone we consider attractive, in that way." she said using one hand to make quotes in the air, accenting 'that way'. "And once you start looking at the same gender that way, you will find you can't stop, it's just… well, natural. We get trained out of it when we are kids. It's not considered acceptable. Yet, if it comes to pass that you start, here you'll find yourself, just like me, wondering what it would be like to kiss you."

I couldn't believe my ears. She was completely reading my mind. AND she wanted to kiss me too! Oh my goodness. Could my body be telling me something I never knew about myself? A warm tingle had ignited between my legs, signifying my sexual attraction. My heart was racing. What was going on!?!

Ashley moved her hand from my leg and lifted her glass. "Kanpai!"

"Kanpai my friend." I barely whispered.

Ashley smiled as her empty glass hit the table. I was sure this smile was unlike any of the others that preceded it.

She took a deep breath, and then blurted out, "So! Do you want to?"

"Do I want to what?" It came out as another whisper. My breath was stuck. What did I want her to say right now?

"Do you want to have a threesome with your husband?"

A frog jumped into my throat. Was I glad, or was I disappointed by her response? My breath released a tiny bit. "Uh...I uh...I don't know. I was just playing around with him tonight, telling him I would. I had been just blowing him off before, whenever he brought it up. I don't know what it would be like, and I think I would be jealous."

"Yes, that happens a lot with first timers."

Was she that experienced to be able to call me a first timer?

"Well, if you ever want to know anything about being with a woman, I will answer anything for you, and never tell a soul. I understand this wouldn't be good for your position as boss here."

"Thank you." I breathed a sigh of relief. I was still a bit concerned about how far this story would go with my team members if it had gotten out.

The alcohol had done its job. My boundaries were blurred, and I pushed on in a direction that surpassed my own safe zone, "So, women are softer?" Why had I asked that? We were out of the conversation. It could have ended there.

"Of course we are, silly. Go ahead, touch my arm."

My breath caught again as I watched my hand drift toward her pale skin. I felt as if I was looking on from a dream. I slid my fingers down her upper arm, then slowed as my hand made its way down her lower arm. I could feel the tiny soft hairs, so silky.

She turned her hand upward as my fingers made their way to her hand. Her fingers moved around mine and gently touched my palm. My clit instantly filled with blood, in its unconscious, animalistic, preparation for stimulation.

I looked up and our eyes meet. I could see her confidence in what was happening. She reached up to touch my face, her hands were so cool against, what must have been, the beet red skin of my blushing complexion.

I reached up to her face as she caressed down my neck and around to the nape. I followed suit and she leaned in for a kiss. My body was completely ready. As her lips touched mine, the fire between my legs exploded, and I moaned softly.

She pulled my head to hers, and used her soft, cool tongue to part my lips. It plunged into my open and accepting mouth. Gently, her tongue fondled my own, then pulled out with snake strike speed. She left my lips with a slight nip to my bottom lip. My body yearned for more, and I leaned toward her.

She did not need any other invitation. She read my body language. Her lips immediately came back to mine and she shared her wet tongue with mine again and again. Her body edged closer each time until finally, she was close enough to reach across with her other hand and grab between my legs.

The moaning escaped me again. How could I have ever thought this would be a bad thing? I was so amazingly turned on by this.

My hips gyrated in sync with her hand movements, rubbing my clit, down and up and back down again. I was breathless. My heart felt like it would slam right out of my chest, and my clit felt like it had swollen to the size of Montana. I couldn't remember ever having been that turned on before.

She pulled me down gently, maneuvered on top of me, all in one swift move. My legs instinctively spread to accept her there between them. Her hand was gone, and it was her warm pelvic bone thrusting against my womanly erection. I could feel the dampness growing in my panties.

"Oh my god." I couldn't stop. It was amazing. She was amazing. Her breathing matched mine as we danced the well-known steps that would lead to release.

She stopped and looked at me. "Are you ok?"

"Yes."

"Do you want me to stop?" She asked and caressed my face again.

"No, absolutely not." I lifted my body up to meet hers, and I pulled her lips back to mine, plunging my tongue into her mouth that time.

She moved her body off me, I groaned with wanting. My body instantly missed her. What was she doing when I had just said more please? Her hands unzipped my pants and I gasped. I cooperated, by lifting my hips to assist her in getting my pants down to my knees.

As my pussy became visible to her, she sucked in air. "Your pussy is just as beautiful as you are."

I didn't know how to respond to that. The next moment I almost screamed. I was taken by surprise and undeniable pleasure as she swooped down, put her mouth around my clit, and forcefully yet gently, began sucking and pulling. Her tongue swept down, spreading my labia lips open.

She knew without a doubt that I was turned on. My juices were everywhere, leaking out of my lips to meet her tongue again and again.

Her hand grabbed my left breast, and with

the slightest pinch of my nipple, she sent chills throughout my entire body. She brought her hand down to my pussy again, she moved her mouth back to my clit, and she thrust her fingers deep into me. I climaxed!

It was far beyond anything I had ever experienced before. My body shivered with sensation as she continued to fuck me. Her fingers were maneuvering to find my G-spot and she focused her attention there. I thought my orgasm was already complete, yet as she suckled my clit and rammed her fingers home, over and over, another outcry escaped me, and my body exploded in pleasure again.

"OH! YES! Fuck me!" I howled.

She removed her fingers and plunged her tongue in. With the heat of my orgasm her tongue felt cool and a whole new sensation of electricity sparked up my body.

She pushed my pants completely off and moved my legs up so that they were above her head. Her tongue drifted down my taint and I moaned with unexpected pleasure. Her mouth was everywhere, my clit, my pussy, around my ass, back to my pussy. My body was shaking beyond control, and she plunged her fingers inside me once again, light seemed to flood my mind. It became more than I could bear, so I reach down to stop her finally.

She laid down next to me and softly caressed

my arm, which sent light tingles toward my spine. She waited for my breathing to slow down, then gave me a light, sweet kiss before getting up to go to the washroom. I didn't know what to think as I lay there covered in my own cum. My body felt like it was floating.

Ashley returned to my side. She brought a warm wash cloth with her, and proceeded to clean me. It was so caring, so gentle, and so foreign to me. I had never had anyone care so much about my experience, and never once had anyone worried about me *after* we had orgasmed. I sat up, and kissed her deeply. "Thank you."

She smiled and asked, "Does this mean you will have a threesome with your husband now?"

I laughed, "Well, only if it is with you. I'm not sure another woman would be able to compare to what you just did to me. It was incredible."

"Why thank you madam." She said pretending a gentleman's tip of the hat.

Chapter 2

When I woke the next morning, Ashley was spooning me. Her soft body fit perfectly around mine, and her silky skin felt wonderful wrapped around me. My first thought was pure pleasure as I remembered the amazing orgasms she had given me.

Then I thought, What about Matthew? I should have been ashamed of what we'd done. I basically cheated on my husband…with a woman. I didn't know how to deal with that. The more I thought about it, I believed Matthew would have loved to have known about it.

I wasn't sure though. Was I just rationalizing, or did I truly believe he would be ok with it, since it was with a girl? I guessed I was going to have to go with that feeling for now. Ashley had said, to deny was to cause undue stress. What could I do about it now anyway? I was halfway around the world, and I felt so good.

Ashley and I were the best of friends since we were basically the only two women in the entire industry, but after that first night, we became a bit more… friends with benefits. We rushed home after work the next day and immediately she tore off my clothes as soon as the door shut behind us. Time and time again she brought me to a climax. Each one surpassed the last. I decided, somewhere in a pause to catch my breath, that I would eventually have to reciprocate. I also had a building feeling that I needed tell Matthew, before it went much further.

It was the week before Christmas. Not that it was apparent in Japan. They do not celebrate that holiday, so there were no decorations, no holiday music. I enjoy Christmas, mostly because of the lights, and there are plenty of lights here all the time, it's just not the same though.

I made my way to my phone booth, taking a deep breath before dialing the number.

"Ok, here goes." I said out loud to myself.

I dialed and waited for him to pick up.

"Hello." he said.

"Hi babe. How was your day?" I asked casually.

"It was good. How was yours?"

"It was good as well. We got a lot accomplished today."

"Enough for you to be home by Christmas?" he asked slightly excited.

"No. You know I won't be. We still have another month of work to do."

"Yes, I know. I was just hoping...hoping to get the best present ever!" he perked up again.

"Speaking of presents," a perfect lead in, "Would you be upset if I started dabbling in the water to get a feel for it?"

"What are you talking about? What water?"

"You know, getting to know...um...a woman…"

He paused. I was unsure of what he would say. It was so difficult to have conversations of a serious nature when you couldn't see the person.

"Are you serious babe? I mean, that would be great! I never thought you were serious about this. I want to say right now that I am so glad I married you. You are the best woman in the entire world!" He was truly ecstatic now. I could hear it in his voice.

My tension left. He would love for me to fool around with a woman, what a perfect world this was, I thought to myself. To him I said, "I know I said we should not intermingle this experiment within our circles, but I found out that one of my team members is a lesbian...or... was for a while or something."

"Oh, wow. Ashley? YES! She is hot, hot, hot! That is who you want to experiment with? That's awesome babe! Have you talked to her about it yet?"

"Well, we kinda had some drinks. We got on the subject of how you wanted a threesome, and she let me know about her past. I ask her what it was like and uh...one thing led to another and…," I cupped the mouthpiece of the phone even though I was in a booth that no one else should have been able to hear me, "...she fucked me."

"YES! YES! YES! Oh man, I wish I was there to see that!" I had to hold the phone away from my head a bit, he was actually screaming. He calmed down and continued, "Ok, ok. Tell me, did you like it?"

I was so pleased that this was going well. I said "O. M. G! I was so excited and wet when she kissed me, I think I almost came right there on the spot."

"Oh ho ho yes! Tell me more!" He giggled with delight, and I envisioned him unzipping his pants. I wanted to make sure actually did that.

"Babe," I said to him, "I want you to pull your penis out for me right now."

Deep chuckles came through the phone.

"Yes, ma'am. Oh, baby are you gonna do to me what I think you are?"

"Yes, sweetie. I'm gonna have a bit of phone sex with my husband five thousand miles away. Trust me."

"I trust you, I trust you. Do me Baby! Oh, my cock is already hard just thinking about you and her kissing. I am so proud of you Babe."

In my mind's eye I saw him sitting on our couch stroking his thick cock with its big vein that runs down the top side, throbbing and pulsing more blood, on the journey to ecstasy.

He asked for more, "Babe, tell me what happened next."

"Yes dear. Well, as I said, I nearly had an orgasm when she kissed me. I was so surprised at how my body was reacting because I was so shy about even talking to her about it, though she promised, twice in fact, that she would never tell a soul."

"Cool."

"So she finished the kiss and started to pull away, and I went in for more."

"YES! I love you babe. Ok, keep going, I'm working on imagining the scene."

I giggled and felt my panties start to get wet again at the thought of what had happened. That, coupled with the fact that it was turning my husband on so much, made me unzip my pants and started doing my own strokes. I moaned, and he moaned with the knowledge of my signature arousal sound. He knew I was actually touching myself right then.

I continued to recant, "She moved closer and used her hand to massage me… down there."

"Oh babe, she touched your pussy? Yes."

"Then she was on top of me, kissing me, her tongue was so sweet. Her pussy was rubbing on mine, and I was tingling all over."

I heard his heavier breathing on the other end, I knew he would not interrupt me with talk again.

"Then she took off my pants and told me what a beautiful pussy I had, just before she put her mouth on it. I think I had a small orgasm right then again, and she just kept going and going, over and over she made me cum.

She sucked on my clit, like she was giving it a tiny blow job, then she thrust her tongue deep into my pussy. I was so wet. My cum was everywhere.

She made me lift my legs up like you do, so she could lick my ass, and then put her tongue even deeper into my pussy. I think I came about 10 times.

Finally, she was finger fucking me and sucking on my clit." I had to stop talking myself at that point, my body was about to climax.

I let him know, "Babe, I'm gonna cum right now."

"Oh, yeah. Cum for daddy. Think about her finger going deeper and deeper into your wet pussy. Spreading those juicy lips open just like my cock. Oh, babe, I'm gonna cum with you. Cum with me, cum with me, oh, oooohhhhh."

My own climax was hitting its pinnacle. I had to stifle my cries to make sure passersby would not hear. "Oh baby, yes, yes, yes. My pussy wants it. Ah, ah, ah." My fingers worked their magic on my clit as I came. My body shook. It was light compared to when Ashley did it, yet the mere thought of her created a better orgasm than I typically could have given myself.

Both ends of the phone were quiet for a minute before I finally spoke.

"Matthew, that was awesome. I think we should have phone sex more often."

"Oh my god babe. You are so hot."

I giggled

Matthew said, "In response to your question, I would say that is a resounding YES!"

"What question was that my dear?" I had completely forgotten how the conversation began.

He chuckled. "As to whether you could play around with a woman. If this is what it leads to, I must say yes. Please do it some more. On one condition of course."

"What is that?"

"Every time you do her, you have to call and

tell me all about it."

I smiled. "The problem with that is, we just spent $50 on this phone call. You might as well be hiring a hooker if I'm going to spend that much every time."

"Well come on babe," he pleaded, "how many times do you think you are going to get to do that?"

"We do live together...with no one else around. I don't know. Maybe I will do her every day. I still need to learn how to please her."

Matthew said, "Ok, ok. Here's the deal then. I agree, you should probably do it some more, get good at it and you definitely need to learn how to go down on her. So, on the day you make her cum, you have to call me about it again. Deal?"

"Deal."

"Awesome! I will let you go, gotta go clean myself up now. Love ya."

"I love you too babe. Chat tomorrow." We hung up.

I slouched back in the seat. My body was still a bit overheated, and the interior of the booth was steamy and musky. I hoped that no one would want to use this booth for a while.

I giggled at the thought of what just happened. I couldn't wait to tell Ashley. I skipped my hot-chocolate, did not walk *slowly* back to the apartment. In fact, I was almost running by the time I got back to the apartment. I thought to myself, I might even give her the old college try tonight.

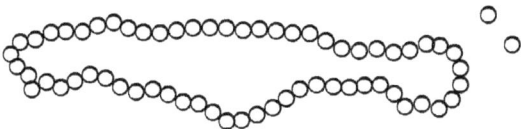

Chapter 3

I bounded up the stairs to our 3rd floor, tiny, home away from home. I was so excited to tell Ashley about the phone call, I knew exactly where it would lead. I went in the door and closed it before announcing, "Honey, I'm home."

My giggle was cut short. I could plainly see she was not home. With barely a separation between the living space and the kitchen, and the sliding doors wide open to the bedroom, as well as the bathroom door being open, I was left to my joy by myself.

I wondered, where she could have been.

We had been there almost two months, and this was the first time she had ever gone out without me. Oh no, had I turned this into a relationship? Maybe she didn't want that. She probably only wanted to give me my first time and be done with it.

I began to brood as I took off my clothes and went to wash out my mostly wet panties. I started to slide into my little silk nighty, which I thought made me look outstanding, then thought better of it. If she thinks I am being too clingy, seeing me in that, when she walks in the door would only solidify the feeling. I opted for soft flannel pants instead.

I turned on the radio, and I found a station that was all instrumental. No need for vocals since I didn't understand the language anyway. Soft sounds, that seemed appropriate for a walk among the koi ponds, calmed my thoughts. I had unrolled my bed mat, and was laying on top of the covers, staring at the ceiling when she came in. I didn't move. Perhaps she would think I was asleep.

She walked over to the bedroom doorway and looked down at me. "How was your talk tonight?"

I couldn't read her mood. "It was great actually."

She went back to the kitchen and unloaded a bag into the fridge. I was a little relieved, it meant she had been to a store, yet I didn't want to push the conversation.

She continued. "Well, are you going to tell me why it was great? That is a pretty unusual answer for 'The Phone Call'."

I was just as nervous to tell her about what had happened with Matthew, as I had been revealing my sexual fling with Ashley, to Matthew. I decided I had just better be out with it and see where it lead. If she was upset or something, I would use some of my extra funds to rent another apartment and be done with it.

"I decided to tell him." I began.

She poked her head out the door dramatically and said with a smile, "...and... What was his reaction?"

I propped my body up on one elbow to turn and face her better. I was smiling now as well. I was so glad to see she wasn't upset with me. "He thought it was absolutely wonderful. I was really not sure how he would react. I had been thinking it was possible that he would think it was unfair, or that I was actually cheating on him."

"Oh, come on. Guys just don't think that way. He probably just thought it was a major breakthrough for you, on the path to him getting his threesome."

I sat up, excited like a schoolgirl, "That's exactly how he took it! You are so good at reading people, it's amazing."

"Yes, I do kind of have that knack. Hey, can I change up the music? Something with a bit more pep?" She said, as she came out of the kitchen with a tub of ice cream and two spoons, one in her mouth, and the other held with the tub. As she sucked the melted vanilla off the spoon I couldn't help but wish it was my clit she was sucking ice cream from.

"Of course." Her infectious good nature had already begun rubbing me right.

Ashley prodded, "So, what exactly did you say?" She found a station that was more like American hip-hop, and continued over to the bed area. She sat down next to me, we both crossed our legs, book casing the ice cream, like we were about to do a séance.

"I was a bit hesitant, and then I asked him what he would think if I 'tested the water'." I used two fingers in the air to quote around 'tested the water'.

She giggled, and continued to use her tongue to fornicate with her spoonful of ice cream.

"He was silent for just a second, I think it was more the shock of hearing me say it out loud, rather than anything upsetting. He was so happy about it, when he did finally speak, he sounded like a kid in a toy store.

He asked me with who, and I said you. He thinks you are the hottest girl we know by the way. I tend to agree."

She bent over and kissed me. Just a quick peck, yet it was filled with coolness and the smell of vanilla. "Keep going." She prodded again, digging into the ice cream.

"He was excited about it, so I ordered him to remove his pecker from his pants and get ready for some phone sex."

Her eyes got big as she tried to swallow and say at the same time, "You didn't! That's so awesome!"

"I did!" I was proud of myself, even prouder that Ashley though it was great too. "I recanted our first time and I've got to tell you, I was so aroused myself, I knew Matthew was getting off, we actually both had orgasms, right there on the phone!" My voice escalated.

"That is amazing! I'm not so good at the phone stuff, too much talking involved for me. So, what happened next?"

"It took a minute or so before either of us could talk again, and Matthew was beside himself happy at the thought. He was even more beside himself at the possibility that you might consider being our first threesome…?" I said a bit abashed. I hadn't really asked her, I had kind of volunteered her, and I wasn't sure how she would react.

"Oh! Sure, I would love to. Matthew's cute, I'm sure if you like his cock, I will too."

I hadn't actually thought about that part.

Matthew would actually fuck her too. Was I ok with him fucking another woman? I shrugged my mental shoulders and thought, I guess so, as long as it was Ashley.

I redirected the conversation, "So, I also mentioned to Matthew that I was going to have to continue with you, so I could...uh...get good, so to speak, and that I was going to need to learn how to please you." I smiled and waited.

Her grin grew into the seducing kind that I knew so well by now. "So...you want to know how to please me, huh?" She stabbed her spoon into the ice cream, and began crawling around the container, cat like, and I knew I would have my wish that night.

"Yes, yes I do." I said softly, and passively laid back so she could pounce on me.

"Well then..." She stopped and got up so she was standing on her knees. "You are going to first need to learn to take charge of the situation." With that, she unrolled her bed mat, and slid into lounge position on her side.

I suddenly realized I had been passive with her every time. I was always pretty forward with Matthew. I guess because she knew what she was doing, I had let her lead.

I corrected myself and followed her instructive movements, turning myself to all fours, The 'Cat Stance' I will call it forever more.

I began to slink in her direction, using the

roundabout fashion, customary to the feline race. "You like your women to be in charge?"

She giggled before nodding her approval.

"Ok," I said, as I approached her feet. "I think I have learned my lessons well, and I may be able to accommodate you.

She rolled onto her back as I flipped my hair and began to sweep up her leg with my silky chocolate curls. Feather like, I was assured by her sudden inhale that I was doing something right.

As I came closer to her pussy, she began to spread her legs for me. I delicately danced, continuing my unique body petting, while allowing her to open herself to me. Her panties were see through enough for me to notice she didn't seem to have any hair.

I brought my mouth down to an inch above her and simply exhaled hot air. She exhaled in response.

I kissed her inner thigh on the right side, then exhaled as I passed over her pussy to kiss her left. She squirmed, trying to raise her pussy to my lips. I kept my mouth just out of contact and exhaled again. That tactic of teasing was one that would typically send me through the roof, so I thought it was a good idea to apply it for this adventure.

With my hand I pushed her short nighty up her belly and I kissed her just above what would have been her hairline, if she had any. With my teeth, I grabbed her panties and began to make my way back down. She obediently cooperated, so I didn't need to struggle too much to get them off, and I flung my head so they would fly across the room, to which she giggled lightly.

Back at her feet again now, she used her hands to prop her head up to watch me, as I swooped in on her foot. I kissed the top of her arch, she inhaled. Then I used my tongue as the body petting device. I slid it first between her toes, making her squirm with delight. Then I repeated the body pattern, a bit faster until I had reached her inner thighs again.

This time, I pushed her legs up and kissed her inner thigh lower, just outside of her outer lips. I could smell her now. Distinctly different than mine, although still enticing in the moment. Again, I swept just beyond reach to her other thigh, exhaling and this time bringing my lips into a pencil size to blow more precisely upon her clit.

At this distance, I could clearly see her clit was protruding, as I had seen mine do when I was aroused. She was definitely ready. Was I?

There was no turning back at this point, I used my tongue to lightly swipe up her clit and she inhaled, then moaned, and gyrated, all at the same time.

That wasn't so bad I thought. I put my mouth

around her swollen clit and gently sucked. Her groan was much more emphatic. I started to play back in my mind, all the things she had done to me that felt so good, and I set out to replicate them all.

I used my tongue to spread her outer lips and glide around the outside. Then I parted her inner lips, they were so soft. Her juices began to come out, running past my tongue and down her ass. Her body was moving with my strokes.

"Yes, that's it. Ou! Stick your tongue in again. Yes, that feels so good." She praised me, and I was so aroused myself although I was determined to make her cum.

I moved myself so I could use my hand to first rest on her clit, then begin massaging in a tiny circle. Her breathing became erratic, she clutched at one of her nipples and licked her lips.

I used one finger to penetrate her pussy gently and slowly. She inhaled slightly and pushed toward my hand. As I pulled my finger out, I joined in a second finger, and went in again. Her exhale came with a bit more volume this time, and she stuck her own finger in her mouth. A sudden image of Matthew's cock sliding into her mouth hit me, and my groin exploded with heat.

Again, as my fingers, ever so slowly came out, I joined a third and went in again, this time with more speed and force, timing it with the music. She groaned and sucked at her finger.

I began methodically pumping my fingers in her pussy. Her juices were flowing and my hand was doused with her. Her hips were pumping to my musically backed rhythm, and I positioned my hand so that the heel would gently tap her clit each time I went in. Her moans grew with intensity.

I felt I was doing well, she was moaning, my pussy was on fire, yet I wanted to make her cum the way she did me. I moved to one side of her body, continuing my finger fucking and then plunged down to take her clit in my mouth. She screamed with pleasure, and although I worried the neighbors would hear, I wanted her to cum harder so I continued sucking and pumping.

With my other hand I reached up and caressed her tit. I pinched it lightly just as she had mine. She reached down and grabbed my head and began moving her hips while holding my head still. The speed built and I increased the speed of my hand and gave her as much depth as my hand would give.

"YES! That's it! Fuck me!" She pumped harder. "Suck it! Suck it like it's a cock!"

I took her instructions literally and began sucking her clit as if it was a cock. Up and down. Pulling it in and out of my mouth.

"YES!"

I could feel her fluids squirting out of her.

My hand continued to pound into her.

"YES! Oh god," her hips pumped, "I'm cumming!" pumping, "I'm cumming!"

Her entire body was shaking. The pumping stopped but I kept pace with my sucking and finger fucking. I know if you stop too soon, it can lessen the orgasm. I opened my mouth and used the flat of my tongue to go down and into her pussy with my fingers. She groaned loudly with delectation.

"Oh yes!"

Her hips lowered to the floor, I slowly pulled my fingers out while sending my tongue in again. Her pussy lips were swollen and resisted my departure. My tongue going in again sent a ripple of aftershocks through her body.

"Oh, my god Terry. I didn't think you were going to be that good the first time. That was crazy good!"

I looked up at her from between her legs and said, "Really? It was really good? Are you sure? Or, are you just saying that to make me feel good? I really do want to learn to do it as well as you do."

"Come here my beautiful lady." She reached for me. I obeyed and crawled up next to her where she immediately gave me a long, full kiss. "I truly mean it. I didn't know. It could be that I like you so much. I have been so horny taking care of you these past few weeks and not really getting any myself, that it was all built up, but I'm pretty sure that was the best head I've ever had, man or woman."

I smiled, moved a bit on top of her to continued making out with her. When I took a breath I said, "You are so hot and *that* was so incredibly hot. When your hips started moving and I knew for sure I was making you cum, my pussy exploded like fire. I think I had a mini orgasm without even touching myself."

She moved me over and propped herself on an elbow. "So, how do you want it to play out when the threesome comes?"

"I don't even want to think about that right now. It's over a month away till we get back. All I want is for you and me to fuck as much as possible, and give each other fire-cracker orgasms over and over again."

She threw her head back with a laugh and came at me. "Well, let's get started then. Someone in the room still has a hot throbbing pussy."

Chapter 4

The next days at work went relatively quick. Most of our work was fast and furious so we didn't have time to think about anything else, luckily. I would have been daydreaming all day about my evenings with Ashley otherwise.

We were definitely beginning to build a romantic relationship. The guys were starting to wonder what was going on as well. We used to go out and get a drink with them periodically, then we just stopped completely. We always had an answer, 'I'm tired', 'it has been a long day', I need to wash clothes' or some such, when in actuality, we were rushing home to have sex.

It was Christmas Eve, it felt so much longer than the short two weeks since I told Matthew. Ashley and I were walking down the street, from the office to our apartment, when someone came up behind me and put his hands over my eyes. Matthew's voice said, "Guess who?"

I turned around in total shock to see him, arms open wide, waiting for me to run into them. My mouth dropped open, I was speechless for a brief moment. "What are you doing here?" I asked, as I regained my composure and hugged him. I looked around for Ashley. This was definitely going to change our afternoon plans. I was immediately aware that I was feeling some bitterness toward Matthew since he had interrupted them.

"Merry Christmas babe! I wanted to surprise you, and Ashley helped me make arrangements and find you. You know, I actually had no idea where you were." He was grinning at me and looking to Ashley for confirmation, then he pulled me into another hug.

My mind was racing. Ashley had helped him do this? She had known he was coming that day?

Matthew continued, "Hey, let's get to the apartment so I can finally stop dragging my suitcase like a tourist. Then we can all go out to dinner, you can show me the town!"

He smiled and we all started walking toward the apartment. Ashley wasn't looking at me. What was she thinking? This threw a whole different ball of wax into the pot. Now I *would* have to start thinking about the threesome. I didn't think I was ready to share Ashley. I'm not saying I was switched over to a lesbian. I could have surely used some real live cock, and Matthew's was a prime specimen to fill me in all the ways I loved, but I'd been happy with my afternoon and evening sexual escapades with Ashley. I didn't want them to change, and they surely would with Matthew here.

Matthew was chatter boxing away, and Ashley was giving him the tour from the surprise location to our apartment. My mind reeled at the possibilities of what was going to happen next.

As we made our way into the elevator, which we rarely took, Matthew turned to me with his big childlike grin, "Aren't you happy to see me?"

I corrected my attitude, like a proper wife, and responded, "Of course I am. I'm just so blown away. This was definitely a surprise. How long are you staying?"

It was probably not the best thing to ask at that moment when he was looking for confirmation of his good deed.

"What? I just got here and you already want to know when I'm leaving?" His humor hadn't died but there was a hint of doubt.

"No, I want to be able to plan accordingly. If you are here for just two days, we have so much to accomplish in so little time. If you are here for two weeks, that's a whole different story. That's all." I leaned over and gave him a kiss to firm up the deal.

He brushed off the doubt immediately and said, "Oh, no, I can't stay two weeks. My boss would have a shit fit. I did manage to get Becky to cover for me for two days and then Mikey is gonna cover another two. Then, with my four days of vacation left, using two days for travel, I have six total...to spend with the two most beautiful women in the world."

His arm had already been around my waist, then he reached over and put an arm around Ashley's waist and brought her closer. My jealousy flared, I'm not entirely sure who I was jealous of or if I was indeed only jealous of one of them. I could actually see a bit of apprehension in the look Ashley gave me. Finally, I thought, she was understanding now why it might not have been a great idea to bring my husband here.

We single filed into our tiny apartment. Matthew stopped to take a broad look.

"Whoa! Talk about a tiny shit hole!"

"Matthew!" I reprimanded. "We don't need any more than this for only three months. It suits us just fine." It was my turn to look for affirmations from Ashley. She was headed to the bathroom as if she hadn't heard me.

"Well babe, it ain't much, but it's gonna be fun." He swooped in for a bigger and better kiss which softened me a bit and I returned it.

When I pulled away I quieted my voice and said in a sort of mock whisper, "Babe, you can't be so forward with her. We haven't really talked about it yet. I thought I had another month to bring it up to her."

"Come on babe, she's been doing *my* wife and *I* have to take a back seat?" He said with a smile.

"No, that's not what I'm saying. I'm sure she will be fine, you just need to be a bit less bull headed, give her some room to breathe, and maybe we can talk about it over some drinks or something. That will loosen everyone up, and I'm sure it will work out fine." My mind was racing. How was I going to pull off the act that Ashley and I were not as intimate as we actually were, and how bringing up the subject of a three-some would be something new to Ashley.

Matthew seemed to understand, and I could feel his body loosen. "Ok, ok. I get it. Where am I gonna sleep? Where do you two sleep? I don't see any beds."

Ashley was coming out of the bathroom now, and I noticed that there was no sound of toilet flushing. "It's Japan big boy. There are no beds like what we are used to. I can sleep by the table and the two of you can have the room."

Matthew didn't want to break up the party, although he did approach it a bit softer this time. "No need for that. I can sleep on one side and you on the other. We are just talking about sleeping right?"

Ashley nodded. "Sure. That works if it's ok with you Terry."

"Yes, that's fine." I knew we were bound for sex sooner than later, so what difference did it make what we verbally decided about sleeping arrangements now.

I pointed to the bedroom, "Matthew, put your suitcase in there. Let's go get some food. I'm famished and we have so much to show you." My Freudian slip left my tongue, and I giggled inside. I saw Ashley's eyebrow move as indication of her humor button getting tagged as well.

As Matthew went in the opposite direction, I motioned to Ashley a silent movie scream, she mimicked back a dramatic, "SURPRISE!" I smiled. Matthew joined us, and we all left to go find a good restaurant that would also double as our drinking den.

Chapter 5

Alcohol consumption is to Japan, what water is to the Ocean. It wasn't a difficult task to find someplace, other than deciding upon what type of food Matthew would be willing to try.

Finally, I made the decision for him and said, "You are going to have to get used to a lot in the next six days. You can't come all the way around the world and then go home and say you ate at Mc-D's."

Matthew stopped abruptly, and swept his hands in front of us for mock protection of some unseen danger. "What? They have the golden arches here?"

"Yes, though if you don't like wasabi, you may want to ask them to put a hold on that. They put it on absolutely everything here, no matter what we call it in the US."

He laughed, and we continued our trek to a local place I liked that had a private room in the back. "That's classic. I do have to eat there, at least once, while I'm here."

I nodded, "Yes dear, I know how much it means to you." His humor was starting to pull me in. It really was one of the things that made me marry him; his ability to have a great time no matter what was going on.

We found a little place, and after some bad Japanese that Ashley and I had picked up, a lot more sign language, and some good old money changing hands, we managed to get into the private room for our meal. Hopefully, it wasn't going to be too much more expensive to have my surprise visit. I knew he had spent at least two grand just on airfare to get here.

After we ordered and got our bottle of sake delivered, I had to usher the table hostess out, promising it was alright not to have someone else pouring our drinks. I introduced my spouse to the tradition of sake.

"Now Matthew, in Japanese tradition, it is not polite to drink alone."

"I can second that." He said.

"Drink rounds are always shared. We all raise and toast, 'Kanpai', and drink the whole shot down. Got it. I'm sure you do." I winked at him to show my humor was coming on.

"Got it." He winked back, and with a bit of difficulty, not being used to sitting at short square tables on the floor, he leaned over and gave me another kiss. "I love you babe. I've missed you so much."

"I've missed you too."

With that, Ashley smiled while pouring round one, raised her glass, and the night began.

The conversation started out politically correct and light. Matthew was backing off, as promised.

Matthew asked, "So, tell me about work. What do you do there? We only ever get to talk for five minutes at a time, and I haven't actually pieced it all together."

"It's not really that exciting to most people I think." I was glad he had chosen light conversation. "You know I have degrees in computer science and some way crazy machinery."

"Yes."

"Well, the whole team is specialized in different aspects of a particularly unique machine. We are actually one of only two teams in the entire world who know how to fix it if it breaks down."

"Whoa! How come I didn't know that? That is huge babe." He changed his voice to his imitation of an aristocrat, "Yes, um, my wife is a mechanical genius, and no one else in the world knows how to do it like she does." He laughed at his own joke, and this time Ashley and I both joined in.

I reached over to get the sake bottle and pour round two. "How is your job going?"

"I don't know that I want to talk about that anymore. I can't believe my wife is a rocket scientist, and she is married to a lowly little car salesman." He chided, "Naw, everything is great! You know me. I am making sales like mad. I made bonus again last month and Sherman is going to take us out to dinner when you get back. He says he's never seen anyone advance the way I have."

"See there babe," I reassured, "I didn't pick you for no reason." Again I winked and he leaned in for a kiss.

I raised the glass and they joined me with a resounding, "Kanpai!" Down the hatch it went.

"What about you Ashley, are you a rocket scientist too?"

She giggled, her amusement was very apparent to me, and I wished we could talk in private so she could tell me what she was thinking. "Yes Matthew, I guess you can call me a rocket scientist too. I'm actually more of a grease monkey though. I really do have a mechanical engineering degree, and I screw nuts and bolts like no one in the world." We all laughed.

Matthew was beaming, "Nice! So Ashley, I don't want to embarrass you in any way."

"I'm sure you cannot." Ashley said confidently.

"Ok, cool. Well my wife here has told me a bit about the two of you and the wonderful thing you have done for us."

I held my breath, I had no idea he would jump into this so quickly, and wasn't prepared at all for this yet.

Ashley giggled and poured another round. "Well of course she did Matthew, she loves you and wants to please you. Our conversation on the subject just lead to an easy understanding of what she wanted to provide you, and I happened to have the experience to teach it to her."

Matthew winked at me, and my tension eased a bit. We raised, toasted and drank once again. Matthew said, "And for *THAT*, I give great appreciation to you Ms. Ashley."

They made mock bows to each other, as much as one could sitting, Indian style, in front of a table.

Matthew continued, "So, to my next...ah... plea for help from you Ashley," he paused, and cleared his throat. Apparently, he was nervous for this next step as well. "We...ah...I was hoping that Terry and I could experience a sexual adventure together."

Ashley smiled. "Well, I would hope you have sexual adventures together on a very regular basis."

He laughed hesitantly, knowing he had been outwitted and I smiled. "Well, yes...ah, I was hoping to have a unique sexual adventure that included a third person...um...such as yourself."

"Well Matthew, why don't we start with a nice dinner and conversation to get to know each other more? You know, like a date. Then, if we all decide that the date went well, perhaps you can come up for a drink after." She winked at me and I smiled. She was putting him in his place for being so flippant, and I loved her even more for it.

Matthew was taken back. He knew he had overstepped by broaching the subject too soon, and he would have to make up for it. "Er...yes, my apologies Ashley. I didn't mean to be so pushy." He lowered his eyes, and I could feel his spirit drop slightly.

I poured another round just as the doors opened and our waitress brought in our food. As she began placing the many small dishes on the table, filled with an assortment of food that would not be too much of a mystery to Matthew, I lightened the vibe by raising my glass, and inviting my friends and loved ones to join me.

We laughed, drank and moved to a position more appropriate for the next event of the evening; cooking.

Matthew was not about to be the next person to speak. He had been put in his place in a very proper manner. It would take a while to get him back to his jovial self.

The waitress lifted the center of the table out to reveal the cooking area below. She deftly ignited the flames. Matthew looked at me questioningly, not knowing that this style of meal meant the food was brought raw, then cooked on an open flame from the center of our table.

I explained, "This is a traditional type of meal that a man would take a woman for on a date. In Japan, the courtship is all about the man pleasing the woman, even when it comes to eating. You must cook our food, serve us, wine and dine us. Then, when a woman accepts a proposal for marriage, after they are wed, the roles reverse, and she takes care of everything for him."

"Whoa. I never would have guessed that for this culture. I mean, I knew women were subservient, I just didn't know we had to woo them into it first." He laughed lightly, testing the waters to see if it was ok to be funny again after his moment of shame.

I didn't want him to look uncultured so I threw him a light laugh as well. Ashely was probably too smart for that though, he had already opened his mouth to insert foot earlier, and hadn't quite removed it with that comment.

"Ok, so I need to do this part. Are you allowed to instruct me?" He got up on his knees in preparation. The waitress quickly glanced up at him with a brief smile. Who knows what she was thinking of our merry little band here. Two women who knew Japan and its cultures, with an obvious tourist who was about to serve both women. I neglected to inform him that in mixed company, the waitress would serve everyone. I was proud of him for accepting the task so easily, and I thought it would turn out much better to have Matthew on the subservient side that evening. Ashley certainly loved to be in charge, as much as I loved her to take on the role myself. We could be the happy couple that pleased her tonight.

I brought my thoughts back to the table with a snap. I guess I was beginning to be ok with the whole situation. Not that I could change it now. He was here. We were here. Matthew had already laid his dick out on the table, so to speak. I'm so glad Ashley gave us more time though. What would we have talked about during the remainder of the meal?

Ashley began food instructions, "Ok, she has placed everything in proper order of how it is to be cooked. The flames will die after a certain amount of time, so this is a timed event as well." Ashley and I laughed at Matthew's look of bewilderment at being thrown into a timed test right out of the gate.

He took the challenge though, and pointed to the right end of the line of dishes. "Do I start at this end? Or the other?"

"First, open that pot on the side there." Ashley said, pointing to what we knew to be a rice steamer. "Use that big spatula looking spoon to put rice in a bowl for each of us."

We both nodded our heads as he looked up for approval. Ashley and I both accepted our bowl with a formal bow. Ashley made a small buzzer like sound when he reached for a third bowl for himself. He looked at her, and she shook her head no. Dutifully, he put the bowl back, and looked to her for his next instruction.

"The meat can go on the grill now, make sure to leave room for the vegetables." She said to Matthew. To me she asked, "Terry, how would you like your meat and vegetables cooked?"

"Yes dear, how would you like them?" Matthew asked. He very rarely called me dear, so I first had to subdue some giggles before I could answer.

"I like my meat on the rare side, same with the vegetables." I glanced at Ashley with a side-ways smile. She knew full well how I liked my food. She and I had served each other before.

Ashley turned to Matthew, "The reason you ask this first, is to plan out where to place everything. Since she likes everything less cooked, you do not want to put hers in the middle of the hot flames."

Matthew was quick to catch on and asked Ashley, "And how do you like your meat and vegetables cooked?"

Smiles passed around the table, and Ashley replied, "I like my meat well, and vegetables crisp." She nodded approval as Matthew placed some meat in the center, and the remainder of our servings more to the outer edge.

There was still a serving left for Matthew and he glanced at Ashley, pointing at the meat with the chopsticks. She shook her head no again. He mimed why.

I replied, "It is not customary for the man to eat until the woman…or women are finished being served, and have tasted everything to ensure it is all to our liking. You are here to solely take care of us and our needs. Once they are met, then you can prepare your own."

He was starting to look a bit doubtful. "I thought you said the heat was on a timer?"

Ashley snickered, "Don't worry, you won't starve. You are doing fine. Time to turn everything over." She instructed, and motioned with a get on with it gesture.

"Yes ma'am." He focused back on the task

at hand, turning each piece before bringing his attention back to us.

Ashley said, "You can get the plates up, everything is almost finished for Terry." Her eyes flashed in my direction. Would Matthew notice that she knew exactly when to bring my food off?

He didn't seem to notice. He got a plate ready and looked back to her for his timing. He didn't seem to miss having sexy conversation. He was calmly taking orders from Ashley, as if it was the most natural thing to do. She really did know how to speak to people in a way that made them feel like everything is alright. I admired her as she guided Matthew through the final steps.

Matthew put my plate in front of me and I took up my sticks to begin tasting. "Hang on Terry, maybe you should wait for Ashley to get hers or something." He looked to Ashley and she again shook her head no. I continued, and took a small bite of each type of food and then gave a bow to Matthew. "Thank you my love."

His face lit up like a kid in a candy store. He didn't need to be told he had made the food correctly. He went to get the next plate set, and I continued eating. After Ashley had tasted each type of her food, she also bowed and said thank you, although she left off the 'my love' part.

With enthusiasm Matthew said, "Alright! Now what?"

Ashley's mouth was full of her last bite, so she pointed at the remaining serving left, and motioned to him. He understood, and began putting his own food on to cook. He looked around the table, being the only one with no eating going on, he seemed to need something else to do. He spotted the sake bottle, and very obedient to his teachings, poured some into both of our cups before filling his own. He really seems to be getting into this serving bit, I thought.

Ashley and I both finished our bites, wiped our mouths, and reached for our glasses. He had already raised his immediately, so he had to linger while we made it to a point that we could drink.

"Kanpai!"

Ashley and I continued eating while he finished preparing his food. The flames were just starting to flicker when he repositioned himself back to his place setting. He smiled to himself, that he had done it in the correct amount of time. He looked to each of us to make sure that he was supposed to eat now.

After his first few bites, he was just as hooked as we were. "Oh, wow!" He said around a mouth full of food. "This is great!"

"I know." I said. "That is why we seem to come to one of these types of restaurants at least once a week. It is always so good. Best part is, it's good for you too. At least now we have you here with us. They seem a bit funny with two women coming in all the time, Japanese women do not usually go out to eat as often as we do."

Ashley corrected me, "We don't go out all the time. I cook at the apartment sometimes."

"Yes you do." I said to Ashley. I admonished in Matthew's direction, "Quite well I might add. We go out, and then she will learn how to do whatever they have done, and reproduce it at home."

Matthew was nodding around his bites of food. He finished a bite and said, "So, you two are Suzie homemakers now."

He might have been prodding for more talk about our 'home life'. I kept it at bay with, "It is quite expensive to eat out Matthew. We really try to eat in as much as possible." I knew I had let the wrong words out as soon as I said them. He had understood, and I could see his mind working on the fact that we were spending a lot right now. Then, he lit up and smiled an evil grin.

He had a low giggle of his own, "Uhuh, I have heard about the eating part."

Ashley laughed. I couldn't help but join her. She had an infectious laugh, and I guess it was time for us to allow *that* conversation to enter. We were getting close to finishing our food, and it would only be a short time before we were walking back to the apartment.

Ashley boldly asked, "Matthew, what is the

most important thing for you to have during your threesome?"

"What do you mean?" He looked perplexed.

"I mean, do you want Terry and I to make out while you watch, do you want me to give you head, do you want to fuck my pussy?"

Matthew's eyes went wide at the blunt suggestions. I clapped my hand over my mouth. I almost spit out my last bite of rice around a stifled laugh.

Matthew looked at me like a deer in head lights. "Uh…I want all of it?" he said with a questioning hesitancy to see if he had answered correctly.

"Ok." Ashley said. "I just wanted to see what your rules were. Some couples have certain parameters they don't want to go past; to make sure their relationship and the threesome are all comfortable."

"You know we haven't talked about that at all." I said to Ashley.

She replied to me and Matthew, "It is actually pretty important for the both of you to have that chat before anything happens with the three of us. I made the mistake of getting involved with a couple before who hadn't laid the groundwork, and it turned into a nightmare."

"A nightmare?" Matthew puzzled. I knew he couldn't understand how having a threesome could be a nightmare in anyone's book. I, on the other hand, could see many possible scenarios that could lead to disaster.

Ashley reached across to the sake bottle, which I was sure was almost empty. She poured another round and said, "I will have one last toast with you, then I'm going to be off."

Matthew started to protest, "What? Wait, no…"

"Yes, it is time for you and your lovely wife to have some time alone together. Never fear, if all goes well with your talk, you will have some ground rules set up, and we can all chat briefly about them when you return, to see where it goes from there." She raised her glass. "To some amazing people, I had a wonderful dinner. Thank you. Kanpai!"

Matthew and I raised ours to meet hers and chimed in.

With the cups empty, Ashley got up, and quietly opened the door, turned to face us, bowed, then closed the door.

Matthew sat stunned for a moment, staring at the door. I reached for the sake bottle to see if there was any left. Swinging the bottle, there was just enough. I poured it evenly between the two of us.

"Matthew." He finally turned to look at me. "One more for the road?"

He smiled and said, "Sure, of course babe."

We raised, saluted and drank.

He put his cup definitively on the table and said, "Well, I hope I didn't fuck that all up. Sorry babe if I did."

"Matthew, she didn't say you did anything wrong, she said we need to speak in private before we do something like this, that's all."

"What are we supposed to be talking about?"

I smiled. "We are supposed to talk, as husband and wife, about what we are ok with and what we are not ok with."

"What do you mean what we are not ok with? I thought I answered that already, I'm ok with everything."

"Matthew," I chastised, "you are not the only person in this relationship."

"Oh! Yes. Sorry. Is there anything you are not ok with?" He flinched with a mock grimace on his face, hoping I didn't say anything.

"I'm not sure. I was definitely jealous when you arrived." I left out the fact that I could have been jealous about sharing Ashley.

Matthew reached over to put his hand on my leg. "Babe, there's nothing to be jealous about. I am yours without a doubt. I would be nuts to give up a woman who would do something like this, you are perfect."

I smiled again. "Thanks babe. I appreciate your appreciation of me. I think any woman would wonder though, why wouldn't you leave me for Ashley. She is just as perfect, in fact more perfect, because you wouldn't have to talk her into this, and she does it all the time apparently."

"What? You are making her out to be a floozy or something." He looked doubtful at that suggestion, or maybe it was hopefulness.

I corrected my attitude. "No, not at all. I'm just saying…as you say, we are both rocket scientists, she is super-hot, and she is so natural with women that it would be easy to conceive of you getting into living with another woman probably. That is hard to compete with, because I don't think I could share you that often." Or her, I thought.

"No worries babe. We are good. I married you, and I'm gonna stick with you. I do love you. Did you forget that?" He leaned in for a kiss again.

The waitress opened the door just then. We probably gave her a heart attack walking in on someone making out. I apologized, and she quickly handed Matthew the bill. I dug out some Yen and slid it to Matthew under the table so she wouldn't see me paying the bill. He got the hint, quickly grabbing it and putting it on the bill. She hustled out so quickly, my body reacted to the expectation of an actual door slamming from our paper separations.

He looked back at me when she was gone. "She was a bit uncomfortable with something."

"Yes, I'm not sure what she thought about

our…threesome dinner. You serving meant you were single, yet she walked in on you kissing me. Not the norm here."

"Oh, oh well. Back to 'the discussion'. So, don't be jealous. I won't leave you if we have a threesome. Is that it?" He asked happily, hoping the conversation was over, and we could 'get down to business'.

"I'm not sure I want you to kiss her. I think that is one of the most intimate things, and it would be nice to keep something for just us." I demurely shrugged my shoulders. I don't know where that had just come from, although it felt right to me. I hadn't even thought about it. I hadn't had any time to think about any of this stuff. I just hope he doesn't feel the same about me kissing her though.

"Sure babe, anything you want. I don't need to kiss her. I do get to fuck her though, don't I?" He might have been getting a bit worried about what he was going to be allowed to do, now that he understood what 'the conversation' was all about.

"Yes, I have been fantasizing about that." My shy schoolgirl smile came across well for him, he perked up at the thought.

"Why Terry, if I haven't said I love you recently, please grab my cock. I believe I'm getting a chub right about now." We shared a laugh. "Are you going to tell me about this fantasy so I can make it a reality for you?"

"Let's just say, I envision her on her hands and knees eating me out while you are pounding her from behind."

"Oooh, yes baby. That's the ticket. How long must we talk about our rules?" He grabbed the crotch of his jeans to readjust his package as it began to fill with excitement.

"Well, our rules are just that you can't kiss her. Other than that, I believe everything else is on the table. Is there anything you want to add to that?" I tensed slightly, hoping he wouldn't add my name to the list of no-kissing-Ashley.

"Nope! That's all I think we need to talk about. I am pretty much open to whatever you are willing to let me do." He smiled, and asked if it was ok for us to go now. I nodded.

We bowed profusely to the waitress on our way out, I was pretty sure I would never come back to this place again, just to make sure of no embarrassing feelings, real or not.

I chose a much longer way to walk back to our apartment, so I could show Matthew some of the sights. I took him to my phone booth and he got a laugh out of it, when I told him how it smelled after we had phone sex. We wandered to the arcade, and he played a game while I coached him on how to play. He was very impressed. They have the best video games.

I decided not to opt for the hot chocolate

in a can for this evening. We would be plenty hot when we got back to the apartment, and even though he didn't say anything about how far we had walked, I could sense that he was anxious to get back. Of course, why wouldn't he be?

When we were just outside the apartment, I turned to face him in front of the door so he couldn't open it just yet. "I love you Matthew."

He smiled with a slight questioning, "I love you too babe. What? Are we not going in now that we are finally here?"

"Yes, we are going in. I just wanted to tell you that in private, before we go to the next level of…um…no privacy."

"Ok, ok. I love you too. It's not even for a whole week babe. It will be over before you know it. Then I will be gone, and soon after, you will be home again." His being gone was not such a bad thought to me. Me being home… I had been calling this home with Ashley. What would it be like, within the relationships I was about to be living? Would it strain my relationship with Matthew, or Ashley…or both? What if I lost both of them?

Matthew bent down to kiss me, he put some passion behind it this time. His tongue spread my lips and he gave me what I wanted; a romantic kiss. My groin began to tingle. When he released me I was ready. I turned to the door, swung it open, and up the stairs we went, two at a time.

Chapter 6

I skidded to a halt at the door to the apartment, and whipped around to Matthew once again. I pulled his mouth down to mine, and he gave me more of what I yearned for from him. I could smell the distinctive scent of his testosterone building. Something I have heard not many are consciously aware of. It turned me on even more.

"Matthew," I said breathlessly when our lips smacked apart, "be a good boy now. Don't waltz in there and assume that she is in the same erotic state as we are."

"I'll be good."

"I'm serious. I can hear the TV on, so that means she's just lounging, watching the boob tube, with no sexual thoughts going on yet. You need to break the ice so to speak."

"Ok, ok. I got it. We haven't been married so long that I have forgotten how to do that, yet."

I nodded, sent one more quick kiss his direction, turned and opened the door.

Just as I knew she would be, she was on the pillows watching TV, although to my surprise, she was wearing a short nighty and the furniture had been rearranged. Our table had been moved across the room, up against the far wall, giving the room wide open space. She had obviously prepared for what was about to happen. Our bed rolls were still in the bedroom, although our pillows had been brought out to the main room.

"Nice!" Matthew said slightly out of breath.

She looked up at us and smiled sheepishly. "Well hello you two love birds. Did you find any dark corners on the way home?"

We looked at each other, realizing we had missed an opportunity. I said, "No, we actually just went and saw some sites, I showed him my stomping grounds, and then here."

Matthew and I took off our jackets, and shoes and came into the room. I unzipped my fly, and headed toward the bedroom with a glance back to Matthew. The noise of the zipper didn't faze him. I'm sure he heard it and knew his task. He was looking at Ashley, getting geared up.

I left the doors to the bedroom open, and made sure to undress where they both could see. Matthew sat down near Ashley and said rather casually, "What are we watching?"

Ashley turned more toward Matthew and said, "I'm not watching anything. I was just passing time." I came back into the room, now in my short nighty. I'm not sure why women always put on sexy clothes just before they take them off to have sex. I flipped the channel so now it was on a music video station, then sat down, right in Matthew's lap. I didn't know how we were going to get this ball rolling, although I felt having at least two of us touching would be a good start.

I didn't need to worry about it though, Ashley did not waste any time, she quickly cat stalked straight to me and started kissing me. I could feel Matthew's cock start to swell below me.

He said, "Now that is what I like. Ladies who get right to business." He was watching over my shoulder, and moved his hands up to cup my breasts. Ashley moved in closer, and he reached out with one hand to make a move on her breast as well, which she pushed into, giving him a hand full.

Matthew squirmed under me as his cock swelled to a size that required an adjustment, so

I moved up onto my knees bringing Ashley with me so we were both facing each other, my left side to Matthew. He would enjoy watching us kiss I was sure.

"Oh, my ladies." he said, adjusting his cock in his pants, and then continuing to give a few more strokes. "You two have got to be the hottest thing I have ever seen in my life."

With that, he got up to his knees as well, officially making it a threesome. He put his arms around, one for each of us and Ashley reached down and grabbed his cock through his pants.

"Oh, wow Terry," she said to me. "I can totally see why you would like that. It feels as big as a coke can in there." She continued to jack him through his pants, and went back to kissing me.

She plunged her tongue into my mouth, and twirled it around mine playfully. Matthew leaned in and slid his tongue into the action. The three of us attempted a tongue battle until Matthew ended it by moving my head to his, leaving Ashley outside the kiss.

She passed the time by continuing her masturbation of my husband's cock, and then used her other hand to begin on me. She slid her hand down my panties and deftly stuck two fingers in my already juicy pussy. A moan escaped me.

Ashley asked, "Terry, can I take your husband's cock out, and put it in my mouth?"

The question sent a new tingle of excitement through my body. "Yes."

Matthew moaned slightly and said, "Oh baby, you are so perfect." He pulled away from kissing me to watch Ashley's hand deftly unzip his fly, unbutton, and then push his pants away from his erect penis, which was dutifully standing in salute.

As Ashley grabbed it again, now with no clothing between her soft hands and his silk like penis, his breath caught. He looked to me quickly, and gave me a very passionate kiss until her mouth slid over the head.

"Ooh! Oh babe. She's sucking my cock." His hand on my shoulder squeezed in pleasure.

I looked down, and watched my lover's mouth slide over the large mushroom head. Her mouth widened to take in more. As she drew back, her saliva left a glistening shine on his beautiful piece. It was another thing I loved about having sex with Matthew, his cock was so big and when it was wet it was so incredibly erotic to me. This was a whole new view for me obviously, watching my husband's wetness caused by another woman's mouth, a mouth that I also happened to be turned on by.

I told Matthew as much, "That looks so hot baby. That sexy mouth sucking that sexy cock. This is going to be some amazing sex, I can feel it already."

Matthew said, "Let me feel it baby." He moved his hand from my shoulder and under my buttocks to slide a finger into my pussy. "Oh yeah! You are so wet. I want to slide my cock in there. I'm not sure I want her to stop that just yet though." His pelvis pumped assisting his piece into her mouth.

Ashley had to reposition to allow for more room in her throat. His pumping action was causing more and more of him to ease into her. I was impressed as to how far it was going already. I don't believe I could get that much of him in my mouth. She was starting to make gagging noises, and I knew that might send Matthew over the edge. The night was way too early for him to cum yet.

Just as I suspected he started to make like he would cum soon.

"Baby…baby…she's gonna make me cum."

Ashley instantly stopped, although not so fast that she didn't give him one last long suck and pull that ended with a pop off the end of his head.

Matthew let out a breath, "Wow, this may be harder than I thought." He laughed, "No pun intended. I mean it may be harder for me not to cum too soon. That was amazing Ashley."

"Well, perhaps you may have to cum more than once tonight big boy." Ashley said with a wink, and turned back to me. "Now, about that cock sliding into a wet pussy, I want to see him do it. Will you let him fuck your pussy so I can watch Terry?" She ended the question by grabbing the back of my neck and forcefully kissing me, her tongue jabbing down into my mouth, and her fingers found their way to my pussy at the same time.

Matthew still had his hand under my butt, a finger thrust in, she joined hers with his. A double penetration of fingers. I moaned from the depths of the kiss, and my body felt like it was turning to mush. Ashley helped by pushing me backward, her and Matthew both guiding me to lay down, my head to the floor. Ashley had moved off to my right side. She grabbed his cock with a pussy wet hand, and pulled him in the direction between my legs.

I spread my legs, and she reached down and spread my lips for him. His cock was so excited I could see it pumping with his quickened heartbeat. He assumed the position and put the head at my entrance.

He asked Ashley, "Do you like to watch?"

"Oh yes. I like it all. Go slow now. I want to see the pop when the rim breaks in and when you pull back, to watch her lips suck on you."

"Oh, man! You are so hot! Yes, ma'am. Tell me what you want, I want to make both of you so happy tonight." Obediently, he pushed himself in until just the head burst into my canal. I cried out in pleasure. Then he pulled back, and I could feel my lips pulling on him, sucking his head, then he was out again.

Again, he pushed just enough to bring the head in and pulled out. It was teasing my pussy, throwing me into ecstasy. "Oh baby…I want more." I pleaded.

Matthew smiled and said, "You have to ask Ashley baby, she's in charge."

We all laughed. I looked to Ashley and raised my hand to her invitingly. "Please baby," I said to her this time, "I want more."

She came down to me and kissed me briefly. "Yes, you can have more." To Matthew she turned and said, "This time big boy, as soon as it pops in, slam it all the way home, and don't stop pumping till I tell you."

Matthew was just on the way out when these instructions came. He shook his head in disbelief with a huge smile, and set his hand to get ready for some real action. His pelvis stopped its backing, and began pushing into my pussy once more. Slowly still, then it was in and he slammed his entire erection deep within me, pounding, and pounding, and pounding, his cock spread my pussy, and juices began to fly.

"OH, YES! Oh….oh…oh…" My screams of passion were harder and louder than I ever remember. His cock was slamming so deep inside me and hitting my G-spot dead on. I was about to cum already. Ashley came down to deep throat my mouth with her tongue and reached under my nighty to fondle my right breast. The left one ached for attention, my whole body was on fire. Her tongue seemed thicker and longer than ever, it really was like a cock sliding in my mouth at the same time, and it heightened the experience. She timed her tongue with the giant cock that was pounding my pussy, my back arched as the orgasm began.

"OH! YES! I'm cumming! I'm cumming! Fuck it harder." He obeyed. My world exploded.

Ashley put a hand on Matthew's hardened stomach and said, "Stop now. I don't want this to be the end for her either." He obeyed and bent down to kiss me. His breath was pumping just as he had. The veins were pulsing on his neck just as I knew the one on his cock was.

Ashley pushed his hips off me as he continued to kiss me, then she positioned herself in between my legs. I could see this shaping up to be the reality of my day dreams. She put her mouth on my hot throbbing pussy, it was so cool compared. She gave my clit a gentle, cooling wash with her tongue, and I moaned around my husband's tongue now in my mouth.

He looked to see what was causing the commotion and smiled as his eyes met Ashley's peeking over the hill of my pelvis.

"Oh how sweet this is gonna be. Is it her turn

to make you cum now baby?"

He turned to look at me, and before he could zoom in for another kiss I stopped him, "Not just me babe. I want you to get behind her and give reality to my fantasy. I want you to stick your cock in her, show her how good it is, how big it is, stretch her pussy open with it, make her cum."

He kissed me very quickly and jumped to obey. He was not going to be asked twice to fuck this little hottie his wife had chosen for him. He would pound that pussy open too, and make her scream for more.

As he positioned himself behind her he said, "Oh baby, this is gonna be nice." He stuck two of his fingers in his mouth to wet them, then put them in her pussy. I could feel her body move with pleasure through her mouth that kept busy pleasuring me.

Matthew informed me, "Her pussy is so wet. Just like yours. I think she wants it."

I asked Ashley, "Do you want it?"

"Umhm." She said without taking her mouth off me.

Matthew kept pushing and pulling his fingers in and out of her pussy. Her breathing was getting heavier.

"Matthew," I said, "Give her your cock now. Slowly and gentle so she can feel every centimeter as it slides in and out."

"Yes babe." He said a bit breathlessly.

He removed his fingers and grabbed her hip. With his other hand he guided his missile to her. Her body pushed toward me as he pushed his large, throbbing cock against her lips. Just as it had with me, his large head popped inside, at the same time her body pulled away from me as she thrust herself on him and moaned. She buried her mouth around my clit again, and began to rigorously suck my miniature penis.

When Matthew had sunk all the way inside her, I again felt her mouth push onto me. As he began slowly pulling it out she pulled with him, although never leaving her task of massaging my clit. Into her, the pushing, away, the pulling, into her-pushing, away-pulling. The rhythm started to increase, and moans came from all of us together.

Matthew was getting to the point of driving in so quickly now that the slapping of skin began. This was a sound that threw me further into ecstasy.

"Yes Matthew, do it harder so I can hear it."

He used his hands to pull her hips toward him and slam himself against her. She had to grab my hips to prevent herself from pulling too far away from me. She narrowed her mouth so she was only sucking my clit now. It truly was like getting my dick sucked.

Her moans increased along with her breathing. I could tell she would cum soon. Her hands dug into my hips and even though she continued sucking me, her focus was waning, being pushed and pulled by my husband's increasing slamming.

I reached down and removed her from me. "It's ok. Cum for me baby, cum on my husband's cock. Does it feel good?"

"Yes Terry. Oh yes. He's gonna make me cum." She moved her hand between my legs and managed to position her fingers up inside me and then braced her elbow on the floor so she could brace herself for the pounding. Matthew was pounding so hard now that even her hand inside me was moving.

"Terry!" Ashley screamed. "Terry! He's doing it! I'm gonna cum." She was at the height. I could see her body starting to shiver.

"Oh baby!" Matthew chimed in. "Baby! Shit. Her pussy is so tight on my dick. She's gonna pull me off." I could see that he was about to cum too. I wasn't sure I wanted this to end so soon, although it's a horrible thing to have an orgasm interrupted, at least for a woman.

"You better be able to do it again, 'cause this is way too hot to stop now." I instructed to Matthew.

I put my own fingers in my pussy to get them wet and began circling my clit. I was so aroused by the entire scene. I could feel my own body nearing another climax.

"Yes, baby! Yes. Oh! Oh!" His head thrust back in the preeminent delivery, and his hips thrust forward, harder and harder. The smacking was loud, the cries of pleasure were louder. I was watching my fantasy in 3D reality.

Ashley cried out with pleasure, and Matthew's body jerked convulsively. His rhythm slowed. Ashley's body sank down to lay on my legs. They were both breathing heavy. Matthew sat back. His erection was still standing strong.

I twisted so Ashley and I both turned over at the same time. Then I got up on my hands and knees and walked backward over Ashley until I was between her legs. I swooped in and began licking up all the juices, her own mixed with Matthew's.

I knew exactly where to go to get her on the path of another orgasm. Her hips started undulating with my sucking. Matthew didn't waste any time, sitting too long would give his penis permission to be done, and he had promised to keep performing.

He got behind me, a replay with switched roles, and slid his cock inside me. I plunged my tongue into Ashley and she moaned again. Matthew's cock did its job and slammed inside me over and over until I too came to climax.

This time, we were all winded and the three of us lay on the cool bamboo floor in a row of sweaty bodies.

I giggled. "Wow. And to think, I had been leery of doing this. Thank you Ashley. Thank you Matthew."

"Oh my god babe. No. Thank you. And you Ashley." Matthew said emphatically. "I used to joke about it with you all the time. I never thought it would actually happen. That was absolutely amazing...hot...sexy. I can't describe it in words."

Ashley simply smiled and closed her eyes. As our breathing evened out, and we all lay there reminiscing, sleep overtook us. Later in the night I awoke briefly and noticed that Ashley had moved to the bedroom.

When I woke in the morning, she was gone. Matthew was rubbing my butt with his morning erection. "Hi babe." He said with a loving smile. "Would you mind if I slid this inside you?"

I was more than happy to allow it. I turned so he had full access to me from the back. He pushed his erection down, and slid it between my legs and I closed my legs around him. Gently he moved between my legs. It caused my pussy to get wet, and as the glide became apparent he used it to bring his hips down and thrust up.

He was pumping inside me again and I was reliving the view of him fucking Ashley. I arched my back to allow him further within. The slapping was getting louder.

Just then, Ashley came in from the hallway.

We stopped and looked at her. Matthew's cock caught inside me and glistening with my juices.

"Oh, hi! Fancy seeing you two like this." Ashley quickly shut the door and came in with a smile.

I said to her as Matthew slowly started to push inside me again, "If you would be so kind as to come join us, I promise to give you as many orgasms as you wish."

Matthew and Ashley both got a laugh out of that, and Ashley quickly undressed, throwing her clothes in a pile near the door and moved in front of me.

"Oh wait!" she said and jumped up and ran to the bedroom. She began making a pile of our bedding in the doorway to the bedroom. "We don't have an American bed, so this will make it kind of the right height in the doorway here with the pillows. Matthew can stand on the living room floor. I want to try something…my fantasy, as it were. Come here, come here." She motioned us over with her hand.

How could I say no when she had been willing to make every fantasy I had ever had come true. "What are we doing?"

Ashley told us how it would take place. "I know it will be a bit rough on your knees Matthew. Terry and I are going to lay on the higher bedroom side, on top of each other. Both of us will have our legs spread and you can be in a position that will allow you to take your pick of pussy." She glowed with delight.

I could see it, and liked the idea. I moved to lay down, face up and Ashley came and laid down on top of me, face down. We began to kiss.

Matthew could see it too. He knelt down and spread both our legs wide and moved between the double pair. He slid his wet cock into my pussy, then slowly pulled it back out. Then, he slid it into Ashley and back out. Into mine, then hers, mine, hers, mine, hers.

Each time he went in Ashley, she thrust her pelvic bone against my clit. It was so erotic. We had to take it slow, the teasing was driving me nuts. His balls would slap against me, then his cock would spread me open. Each time was like the first time, that thrill of tingles would shoot through my body.

Ashley and I were heatedly making out. I loved sucking her tongue like a blow job and when I thrust my tongue into her mouth she moaned with pleasure. I think she really wanted another cock involved.

As we writhed beneath Matthew I could feel his tension. He wanted to cum.

"Ok Matthew." I said breathlessly. "Cum baby."

He had just thrust inside of me. He lay over on us, and continued his doggie style thrusting into me. It only took him a few seconds and…

"OH! YES! Fuck!"

Matthew slowly pulled out of me and sat back. Ashley kissed me a quick peck. "Well, good morning." she said.

I smiled up at her. "Why, yes it is."

She got up and headed toward the bathroom. "I hate to break it to you, but in Japan it is a work day." She disappeared into the bathroom, and I got up to get dressed myself to be about the business I was here for.

Matthew grabbed a pillow from the pile, and lay back in the middle of the floor with a huge smile on his face. Arms and legs spread in proper snow-angel creation mode. Ten minutes later, Ashley and I quietly closed the front door as Matthew slept; a smile on his face.

Chapter 7

The next 5 days went by in a flash of hot sex, cum and juices everywhere. The three of us continued the after work ritual Ashley and I had begun before Matthew's arrival. I did make a point to make sure that the three of us had dinner with the team twice while he was there, just to make sure it didn't look too suspicious.

After Matthew left, things with Ashley and I returned to some normalcy. There were only three weeks left of the contract. Ashley and I continued our lesbian pleasures daily. I will totally tell anyone, any time, that I truly loved her. I wanted her to come stay with us when we got home, and I told her as much.

"Will you come home with me?" I looked at her out of the corner of my eye as I chopped some carrots for dinner.

She was quiet though, thinking to herself. It drove me nuts when she didn't answer me right away. Every time I brought this up she would go all quiet on me. I wanted an answer this time. We were due to leave soon, and I wouldn't be able to stand the 'not knowing' if she didn't tell me before we left.

"Ashley! What are you thinking?"

She looked at me briefly, took a long, slow breath, "I'm not coming home."

I was stunned. She really was going to end it. How could she do this? ...to me as her lover, and me as her boss? I put the knife down and leaned into the counter to steady myself.

After an impossibly long moment she said, "I took a position with Yoduki. They offered me a great package if I would stay on and manage the department. I didn't know how to tell you." When she realized I wouldn't say anything she continued, "I know I should have told you sooner. I'm sorry. I should have ended it between us as soon as I found out...to lessen the pain."

Hot air seemed to shoot through me, lessen the pain? What? Pain is pain, it is either there or it is not.

"Terry?" She had come to me and put a hand on my shoulder.

My tears sprang up uncontrolled. Her touch had turned on the faucet. I didn't want her to see me cry, it was unfair of her to do this to me, leaving me in such a mess. I couldn't look at her.

"Terry, I'm sorry." She softly left the apartment.

When I had my waterworks under control I looked around and noticed for the first time that most of her things were already gone. She had known it was coming. She had prepared for this moment. Coward!

She never returned to the States as far as I know. I was definitely sad for a while. She hadn't even showed up for our last two days on the job. I didn't know what to tell the other guys other than what I knew, "She somehow found time to go through a job interview here."

I had thought we spent every waking minute together. I guess it had all just been wishful think-ing on my part, that she wanted to come home and be with us forever, a poly relationship. At least with me… Maybe I was correct months ago when I had a feeling that I was being too clingy with her. Maybe she knew it wouldn't last.

I am glad for it now. I'm not so sure I could have lived like that forever. Being that different in our society is not an easy thing, it would mean hiding how we lived from everyone we knew. She had said to be yourself, always, no matter what other people thought.

Thinking back on those few months gave rise to many nights of pleasure in our house after my return home.

Chapter 8

I had to replace Ashley of course. At work, I mean. Every time I interviewed someone though, it brought it all back. I'm not sure that it was a good thing that I thought of her so often. Some interviews would end with me in tears, and others would end with me rushing out of the office to go home so I could fuck Matthew.

I was a wreck. It was unlike me to behave like a schoolgirl with her first crush. I think the guys knew something was amiss. I was hoping they thought I was pregnant or something. Sam even tried to pull me aside one day and open a conversation about it. I deftly avoided it of course…for a while.

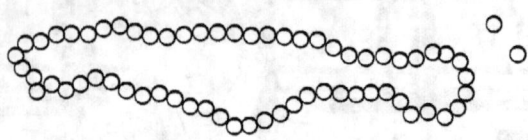

Sam had me pinned under The Machine. I should have known he was up to something when he asked me to do something so easy.

He eased onto the path he had orchestrated, "So, what's going on with your life Terry?"

Don't bother beating around the bush anymore, he's got you. "I'm just stressed. I don't like us working shorthanded, and these interviews are pissing me off." Some of it was the truth.

"Ok, ok. Tell me what I can help with." He knew exactly how to calm me down. "What if I play your receptionist for a while?" We both laughed.

I raised an eyebrow though, "That actually doesn't sound like a bad idea. You may have just stepped in some…"

He grumbled like he hadn't expected me to take him up on the offer, although his grin showed me he was happy that he had lifted my spirits. He feigned displeasure, "Awe man."

Just then the phone rang. We both looked at each other. I stood my ground for two rings, he jumped to a run when he realized I was completely serious.

I heard his voice from my office, "Denchek Technicians, this is Sam. How can I help you?"

Wow. He's good. I should have had him doing this all along. If he can filter my calls that will save me loads of time. I went back to my day and was in a very chipper mood when I arrived home that evening.

"Honey! I'm home."

From the living room, "Hi."

He tried to look around me to his TV show as I jumped on his lap and bounced. Distractedly he finally chuckled and looked at me. "What is all this about?"

I smiled and gave him a quick kiss. "I don't know. I'm just in a good mood for once. I hired a new guy named Timothy, finally. We won't be shorthanded on the next contract. Sam is going to start filtering my phone calls so I have more time for admin stuff." I paused for a breath, "I'm just… I don't know. Do you wanna fuck?"

He glanced at me, then back at the TV again, "Yea, sure."

I pulled back slightly, "Sure?"

"Yea. What?" He continued to watch TV.

I climbed off and stood in front of the couch looking down at him.

He glanced up momentarily. "What? I said yes."

"Well…? You either do or you don't. If you do, I would imagine it would be best if you STOP watching TV and get to it."

"Damn babe. There's only like ten minutes left. You go get undressed, and I'll be right there." He didn't even glance at me.

I paused for another second, unbelieving, then turned and walked away. I can't believe I was finally truly in the mood, and he was going to kill it like that. Fuck him!

Two months later Timothy was whining in my office about going on the contract. I knew he wasn't married. And now that it was almost time to go, he was distraught to leave his new girlfriend for six weeks. As the boss, I was a bit perturbed. It took months to train someone.

"Timothy, you knew coming into this we go on extended contracts. If you don't go, you are putting us in a jam. That puts all of us at risk. You know that."

"I uh… I know. And I'm sorry. It's just that she said she would leave me if I was gone that long."

I looked down at my desk to calm myself.

"I don't want to be involved in your personal life Timothy, but this is the job. You signed a contract with me, and I have a contract to fulfill that requires the services you agreed to perform. You have been here for two months training for this and now is the time when we make our money. On contract!"

"Yes ma'am."

He was getting under my skin. Everyone knew I hated being called ma'am. "Timothy, what do you want to happen here?"

"I need to be excused from this contract." He wouldn't even look me in the eye.

"Timothy, if I excuse you from this contract you will be in violation of our contract. You will lose your job, and you will owe back all the pay you received for the past two months."

He looked at me, stunned. I saw his mind trying to wiggle out of this decision. On one side was his heart and on the other, a very well-paying job that was difficult to obtain. "Um… can I talk to her and let you know tomorrow?"

I sucked in air through my teeth, rolled my eyes and said, "Sure." I can't believe the stupidity of people. I know what his answer will be tomorrow and even if it isn't, he won't work up to par. I have to let him decide though, otherwise I forfeit the money I've paid him.

I must spend more time on the hiring process for the next one. It is just too expensive to train someone who won't stick around long enough to make their pay back.

Matthew whined, "Interviews again? You are so crabby when you are looking for staff. What's the big deal?"

I paused to really look at him. How could I have been so stupid? What made me think this man was a perfect fit for me? To him, "It's because of the time away from home. So many people are not accustomed to that. These people are also ridiculously smart, although not so much in the way of everyday life stuff. Then there is the fact that not that many people in the entire world have the correct qualifications."

"You should quit this job babe. It stresses you out too much."

"Quit? I own it. I can't quit."

"Oh, yea. I forgot about that part. Well, sell it or something."

He walked out of the kitchen with his beer in hand, and I was simply stunned into silence. Just sell it or something, so fucking easy, just like that. What an idiot.

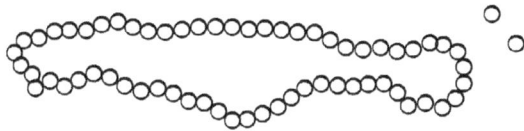

Sam let my next appointment into my office, Brian. I would be focusing on carefully prodding for some personal information this time, it really was pertinent to the job. It was a touchy situation though. Legally you are not allowed to ask those kind of questions. Brian was the best choice at the end of a list of candidates. I couldn't wait for any more interviews. We had a contract coming up in three months and I needed to get someone in and trained. I hoped my eyes were not glazing over as he rambled on about how qualified he was. He had the air of a man who thought highly of himself. I got the feeling he thought his intellect was above mine.

Don't ask me why there were no other women in this field. I think women would be better suited for it, for sure. At least they would come in with some modesty in the beginning.

I hired Brian. No one else was even close to qualified. Where did I need to go to find the right person? I called all the universities and put ads in just about every paper in the nation. I didn't want a foreigner.

Brian and I didn't mesh well. We were on our way home from contract and I knew already, I would have to fire him. Our team needed to be a smooth, well-oiled operation. Brian just didn't get it. He questioned everything with negativity. He didn't take my directions, and I found out that he had blamed Rick for one of his mistakes. This contract was the worst ever. The rest of the team pulled together. We had to spend two extra days on site to finish, something we had never done before. I finally sent Brian home, and we finished earlier than we would have, had I kept him. That decision actually made the rest of the team happy. They hadn't said anything out loud, although I felt they were doubting my abilities as a leader. Or at least my ability to find a new team member that worked.

I opened the door to our apartment and find, yet again, what looked like a fraternity had partied there. This is getting old. Every fucking time I go away he digresses and then I have to come home, tired, and clean up *HIS* mess. He needed to get a fucking life! A new life without me.

He was nowhere to be found. I began the

drudgery of cleaning. I didn't even take my coat off.

I needed to change my life.

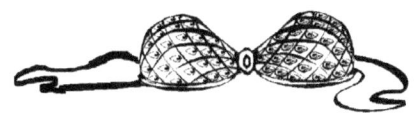

The next round of interviews. The last of five had left about an hour ago and I sat perplexed at my desk.

Sam was leaning on the door jamb with his arms crossed watching me at my desk when I look up. "Hey," he said.

"Hey to you too. What's up?"

"I just thought you might need someone to bounce ideas off of. You look like you are having difficulty making a decision this time."

"Yes." I chuckled at the thought of my dilemma. "I am so amazed that I found two to choose from. They are both equally qualified for the job. Isn't that the kicker? Three rounds of interviews and all I get are idiots, and now I have to make a choice between these guys."

He came in, and sat in a chair across from me and grabbed a notepad and pen. "Ok, what are their names?"

"Steve and Trevor." I smiled. I was beginning to feel really dependent on him.

"Education...?"

"They both have identical education. In fact, there are very few differences in their entire resume. They even went to school within a year of each other, one in Cali and the other in New York." I shook my head in repeated disbelief.

"Wow. That is interesting. Well, New York is a better school. Who went there?"

"Trevor."

"One up for Trevor then. What have they been doing since then?"

"Both have been meandering around in crap jobs that didn't need their skill sets. They are like twins or something."

"Ok, let's get to their personal life, because... well...that is really important to us."

"Yes. Go ahead, rub my nose in it. I did ask the last two, and Brian, well that was nothing to do with his personal life."

"Yea, that just had to do with the giant stick up his ass." We both laughed and shook our heads.

I held both resumes up in front of me and glanced at each in turn. "I don't know. Steve is great. He kinda reminds me of you in a way. He has a very caring nature, he's older than all of us. His wife passed away, and I got the impression he has it set in his mind that he will never love another."

"Oh, one up for Steve then."

"Trevor is younger than all of us." Sam grimaced at that and I nodded a slight agreement. "I know. We don't have the best of luck with the young ones. They fall in love."

"Yea, what kinda crap is that?" His sarcasm lightened my mood even more.

"His energy is awesome. He likes to joke around. I think we need a little more of that at the moment…after my pissy mood for the past year. He has strong leadership qualities…he seems like a mini-me actually."

He made a tsking noise, "You're telling me."

We nodded and the look of deep thought furrowed both our brows.

I saw the light in his eyes go on. "You know," he said, "I do believe I have the best answer."

His dramatic pause made me smile, although I really wanted the answer now so I could be done with this. "…ok do tell…"

With a devious grin he finally answered, "Hire them both!"

He confidently smiled while I digested the thought. Why hadn't I thought of that? I could definitely afford it. I might actually be able to take some time off…once I am confident they are properly trained of course. I looked at Sam, so smug. He knew it was the perfect answer.

Sam said, "Hire Steve to replace Ashley finally. Hire Trevor…to replace you."

It's like he just read my exact thoughts. Is

it so obvious that I want time off? "Ok. You're right. Let's do it. Get them both on the phone, ask them to come back in."

He jumped to the task, "You got it boss lady."

I don't know if it was my mental thought to change or the Universe just decided to stop fucking with me.

Steve was great. Very attentive to learning. He was so appreciative for a job where he could finally use all of his training. He and Sam hit it off right away and Sam took it upon himself to tutor him. Yet another way Sam picked up some slack for me, I loved him for it.

Trevor really was just like a duplicate of me. He had a knack for lifting the spirits of the whole crew. It increased our productivity. I was so grateful to Sam for suggesting the dual hire. I spent a lot of time with Trevor training him into my role as a leader, as well as tech support.

I went with them on Trevor and Steve's first contract. Turns out I was only needed to oversee. It was strange for me to be just standing around.

Sam got on my case one day when I pitched in and started helping. I was completely bored though, and tried to keep helping. He reminded me we needed to make sure the new team could operate without me. I pouted comically, yet deep in my heart I really was pouting. This was my baby, and here it was growing up and moving on without me.

Two years flew by. They had once again become a perfectly functioning team, they worked seamlessly together. The team had been gone for three weeks. I had decided to stay home this time. I knew they would be fine. Besides, I needed to figure out if I could salvage my marriage or not.

I had only been going into the office for about 20 hours a week while the guys were away. There was not much for me to do by myself, and the shop felt cold and empty without them.

At home I was playing the good little wife. I made Matthew breakfast, packed him a lunch, and always gave him a kiss at the door. I cleaned the house before I went in to the office to do my minor bits of admin. I organized my closets, bought some new clothes, and watched some day-time TV during the rest of that contract. (That was totally weird. I can't understand why people do that.) Then, shopped, cooked dinner, and waited for him at the door.

Matthew was rather startled by all of my

attention at first. He did not say anything out loud about it though. I'm not sure what he thought. After dinner we watched night-time TV, and then we'd have sex. It was all blasé however. I did it because I was trying to live a somewhat normal life. He never initiated any kind of foreplay. The first couple days he had been very excited when I offered a blow job as foreplay. Now, it was an established routine. He would simply shut off the TV and we'd go to the bedroom to have sex. Wham, bam, not even a 'thank you ma'am'... Where's the lube?

One weekend I tried mixing it up. After I had cleaned up the dinner mess, I told him I was going out. He barely seemed to hear me through his TV program. He just said "ok, see ya." I couldn't believe that was it. Here I was trying my damnedest to make a go of our marriage, and he truly seemed to not care one iota. I went out by myself.

I had no idea where I was going. I hadn't been out by myself in years. Matthew and I only went to Finnegan's for the occasional beer and appetizers. I didn't want to come home and just sit next to him on the couch, so I stayed out until the bars shut down. He was asleep when I got home. He never even asked me about it.

Chapter 9

Sitting on the couch now, deeply entrenched into the doldrums of our 'scheduled' late-night TV. I can't wait until it's over and he's asleep. I think about my day tomorrow. I have more interviews to do. Trevor met someone last year and they got married, and were now pregnant. Damn him. Or should I thank him? I'm not sure. It will be awesome to have to go away on contract again, if I don't find someone to replace him in time. I snickered to myself, then squashed it, hoping Matthew didn't hear me, and want to know why I was laughing.

The guys are getting restless to have the gap filled of course. It has been six months. I can still do most of the physical work, even though I'd gotten into a routine of letting the team do most of it. I just don't want to keep up the pace of filling two positions any more. It was so nice to only have to be the boss. I could do all the administrative stuff and not worry about the manual stuff. It's wearing on me, and on them. Hell, it's taken my marriage to the very edge. Matthew just doesn't understand when I say I'm tired, I really am. He thinks I'm lying. Maybe he thinks I'm having an affair or something. Good. How did I get all this stuff done before I had Trevor? Luckily we haven't had any away contracts.

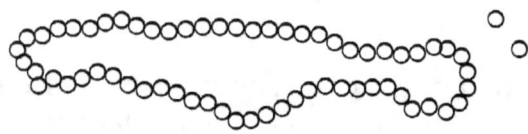

Steve came in the office. "T, your next interview is here."

"What do you think about him?"

"He's young. That's about all I can say so far. He doesn't talk much."

"Ok, send him in. Name?" Digging through papers, I tried to find the file for this guy.

"Jeremy. I had to dig it out of him. He only wanted to be formal with me." He imitated, "Mr.

Tellesh, sir." He scoffed, rolled his eyes and went to fetch my next prospect.

Found it. Jeremy Tellesh. Scanning through his resume, I'm quite impressed. If he can perform as well as his credentials say he should, we may have something here. The 'shy thing' would have to go though. You have to be able to talk openly with everyone in order to be part of this family.

He was tall, thin and dressed very business-like. I stood to shake his hand when he entered, and motioned him to the seat across from me.

"So, Jeremy."

"Yes, ma'am. Jeremy Tellesh."

"If I decide to hire you that will be the first thing that has to change. We do not stand on formality here. This operation can be a bit dangerous and we all work together like a family."

"Yes ma'am."

"Tell me about yourself." I hated people calling me ma'am, since this was still interview time, I needed to establish who was boss, so I let it slide.

"Um. I have a degree from DeVry University in general engineering…"

I interrupted him, "No Jeremy, I have your résumé, and I have read it. I want you to tell me about yourself. As I said, we work very closely. We have contracts where we live together for four to twelve weeks in hotel rooms. I need to know about *you*."

He paused, unsure. "Uh…oh, ok. Um… I don't really have a lot going on. I have been doing dual degrees for so long. No time for much socializing."

"Have you had roommates in the past or currently?"

"Yes ma'am. I have been living in a three bedroom house with two other guys for the past four years. Before that, I lived with another guy." He seemed a bit perplexed at how that sounded coming out of his mouth. "Uh…I'm not gay, or anything. We're just roommates."

"Doesn't matter to me. It might to the other guys you will be living with when we are out on contract though" I smiled to lighten the mood. It was a joke. He seems nervous, good.

"Ma'am, I am actually, usually, very good at communicating with people. My skills far out-weigh the requirements that were listed for this position, and I would welcome the challenge both the technical, as well as, meshing with your family."

I liked him. Once he got passed his shyness, or nervousness, whatever that was... I decided to go on a hunch.

I nodded. "Let me introduce you to your new family."

I left work early so I could surprise Matthew. I was in a great mood, having found who I thought was the perfect person to finally fill the team again. Just in the nick of time too. We had a pending contract. I would get to go away again, and only have to be the boss.

I knew it would be a lot to get Jeremy up to speed in less than two months, although he seemed up to the task. He was definitely devoted to 'the challenge' as he said. The rest of the guys understood it would mean more pushing from them. Knowing we would be whole again inspired them. They all seemed to take to Jeremy immediately.

It was time to go home and be a good wife, before I had to break the news that I would have to go on this next contract. Trevor's pregnant wife was due during that time, and Matthew didn't know I had hired Jeremy. It was a perfect excuse.

It would be the first contract I had been on in years. I don't think I could admit it yet, but, when I was offered this contract, I was already contemplating the reality of the end of my marriage. We didn't even have decent sex anymore, and the rest of our coexistence was just that, more like a business arrangement. We each had our tasks to accomplish to make our lives run smoothly, and we scheduled our sex as part of that plan. The passion and spontaneity that Matthew had with me in Japan was long gone. Looking back, I couldn't even put my finger on the specific moment when it started to happen, the slipping away from each other. The only way I could make myself climax anymore was reliving the memories of Japan, and Ashley.

When the contract came, I lied to myself. I thought, it won't hurt to have some time away again and, who knows, perhaps something similar will happen to spice up the passion again somehow.

I was bouncing around the house when he got home. I had dinner cooking, his favorite. I had put on my 'I want to fuck' outfit as well. A skimpy little slip made of silk. It barely covered anything, and was see through to boot. One last hoorah to see if he would get romantic.

He came in. I bounced over to where he could see me and made a dramatic pose.

He barely noticed me. "Hey babe." He waved a flippant hand, then disappeared into our bedroom.

Well, that didn't go as planned. I went back to the kitchen to finish getting everything ready.

"Babe? Are you hungry now? Do you need a few? I cooked bacon wrapped, filet mignon."

He called from the bedroom, "Oh. Sorry. I ate on the way home. I didn't know you would be here."

I stood with my hands on my hips, stunned. Wow. What a waste of all this food? "Oh. Ok. Yea, I guess I should have called you. I just wanted it to be a surprise."

He came out of the bedroom and got a beer out of the fridge before even looking at me. "It was a surprise. What has you Whoa!" He paused as he raised his beer to his mouth, "What has you all spunky? Damn, I wish I had known we were having sex tonight. I am meeting Will in like… 30 minutes."

He took a swig of his beer, and sauntered over to me. "I suppose I could pull off a quickie before I go though."

His smug smile pissed me off. I rolled away from him slightly as he tried to kiss my neck in what felt like a sleazy way. "Yea, sure babe. Whatever."

"Hey! It's not my fault you didn't tell me. I could have cancelled if I had some notice."

"It's that important that you meet Will? Come on babe. We haven't had much time together, and I'm trying to make it up to you. What is Will doing for you?"

"Well…" He chuckled. "Not that! All the

guys are getting together to watch the game, and I have bets down."

He kissed my neck as my body unconsciously pulled away.

His voice heightened. "Tell you what. I'll leave early if it looks like it is a for sure, one way or the other. The guys will understand if I tell them what you are wearing, and that you are waiting for me." He loved his idea.

He pecked another kiss on my cheek and let me go. Ugh!

He went to grab his coat. "I'll see ya in a little bit babe. Wait up for me. We will make up for lost time." With that, he was gone, and so was my marriage.

Weeks went by before I finally got around to telling him I was going on another contract.

Chapter 10

The next five weeks went by quickly. We had a lot of things to do to get Jeremy up to par. He picked them up faster than I thought possible.

Rick and I were working on the back end of the Tammy. Ken and Sam were teaching Jeremy the intricacies of our next contract; by first showing him how to break our tester device, which we affectionately called Tammy.

Steve came over and said to me, "T, you need any help with that?"

I looked back at him with a goofy smile. I had been pulling on this wrench for a good three minutes, it was obvious that he had been watching me. "Yea, sure big guy! Get your hands dirty."

He smiled wryly, "Oh, I wasn't offering my help. Hey kid! Get over here and help the boss unlock this damn nut."

Everyone looked over when Steve called out. Jeremy looked at Ken & Sam who both nodded to him. He jumped to obey. The guys were having it out on both of us. Me for not having the strength to get it off, and Jeremy for jumping when 'the boss' needed help.

I was half under the butt of Tammy. I had slumped back when rescue had been offered, though I couldn't really move out of the way.

Jeremy knelt down next to me and it became awkward when he needed to reach across my chest to grab hold of the wrench. I felt a strange tingle of intrigue as he did. I caught a whiff of his sweat mixed with oil and noticed his young, bulging arm muscles. I was shocked to be so suddenly aroused.

He adjusted, and braced his legs around me. I could feel all the other guys snickering. Jeremy had no idea he and I were the butt of a joke now. He would soon enough. They wouldn't let him forget he had the boss between his legs.

I looked up at him with my grease smudged cheek and started to laugh. All but Jeremy joined me. He had a determined look on his face and the nut broke loose finally.

He looked down at me with a look of pride in his accomplishment. Our eyes locked. A moment of…something…was between us. He smiled, not realizing my grin was in humor of the situation more than approval of a job well done. For a moment time slipped.

The phone rang. I jumped back to reality as Steve went back to the office to answer it, still laughing.

Jeremy said down to me, "Did I do something funny?"

"You and I just became the butt of a joke that you will *never* be allowed to forget. That's all."

"What?" He looked around at Rick, Ken and Sam, imploring. Rick made an obscene gesture, stroking his air-cock down an invisible mouth. They all erupted in raucous laughter.

Jeremy jumped back from me. "I'm so sorry."

I laughed harder for it. I turned over, wiggled out from under Tammy and extended my hand to Jeremy to help him get up. A tingle of pleasure ran up my arm as he grasped my hand. God, he was handsome.

Steve called out from the door of the office, "Big T! You gotta phone call. You have time, or you need a message?"

"I can get it. Give me 30 seconds."

He went back into the office to place the

caller on hold. Jeremy was still pleading with his eyes for me to forgive him. I patted him on the back and walked away laughing. The guys took turns giving him a pat before returning to their work.

I picked up the phone before I sat at my desk. "Yes? This is Mrs. Denchek. How can I help you?"

"Mrs. Denchek. This is Rachel Cornswall. My employer would like to make an appointment with you to make an offer on your company."

What? The pause was longer than my brain normally takes to process information. "Excuse me?"

Lobell Technologies has been following the progress of your company, and feels it would be a valuable asset to their portfolio. They would simply like to arrange a time to meet to discuss whether you are open to a merger, or possibly a complete buy out."

"I hadn't put any thought to it before."

"If we can set a time next week, that will give you time to process, then you can discuss it with Mr. Lobell. Is Monday or Tuesday better?"

"Tuesday." I answered automatically without giving it much thought.

"He is available at either 10 am or 3 pm, which would your prefer."

I suddenly snapped out of being led by my nose. "Neither. I am only available at 12 noon."

"Thank you Mrs. Denchek. Mr. Lobell will arrive just prior to 12 noon. Have a wonderful day." She abruptly hung up.

I penciled in the appointment to my calendar, still in disbelief. What kind of business has such an amazing receptionist? Someone wants to buy my company? Do I want to sell? They have been following my progress?

I went back to work and didn't put another thought to it…Until Tuesday.

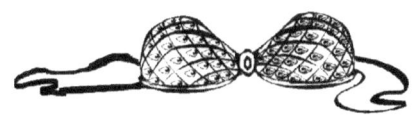

I couldn't believe I hadn't even thought about it.

"Terry!" Rick shouted at me.

I snapped out of my thought and grabbed the release valve to stop the flow of pressure from escaping. "Sorry Rick."

"We need to take a break. You almost got your face burned off."

"Yea. Let's take a break. I have a meeting at noon. I need to gather my thoughts before then."

Rick looked at me with more than just a little of concern as I walked away.

Back in my office, I looked up Lobell Tech. A huge conglomerate company that buys and sells the little guys. They will gobble my company up and spit out…what? I will tell this guy to take flight. Too bad. The idea of not having the stresses I have had for the past couple years sounded nice for a brief second.

Mr. Lobell arrived as promised, five minutes before 12 noon. I watched from my video surveillance camera as he got out of his stretch limo. He was followed by not one, but two assistants with briefcases, all three dressed in black suits.

I heard the door close and purposely waited two minutes to come out of my office. As I took two carefully planned steps out my door and stopped, I extend a hand, waiting for him to come to me. "Mr. Lobell."

"Mrs. Denchek." He crossed to me and shook my hand. "Thank you for seeing me on such short notice. I am sure you are extremely busy. I believe you have a new contract you will be leaving for shortly and need to prepare?"

I stared directly in his eyes. I didn't respond. My contracts were typically confidential, since the machines were often in classified areas. "Please come in." I spun on my heel, and lead him into my office.

His assistants followed. Mr. Lobell took the closest seat. His assistants stood back behind him. I did not typically have a lot of people in my office so there was only one other chair in the room. I guess if there isn't enough for both, they must stand.

I began the conversation, "Mr. Lobell, I have to admit, your inquiry took me by surprise. I have not thought about selling my business. Aafter reviewing your company, I am not sure I would consider selling to someone who would perhaps dissolve my company."

"Perfectly understandable Mrs. Denchek. I know what the internet says about my company, although, I can assure you we do not purchase companies that will be dissolved. I only purchase a company if I have a need for it."

"And what need is that?"

One of his assistants placed a document on my desk he said, "Over the past six years, you have serviced nine devices that my company owns. It's simple mathematics."

I looked at the document and saw the names and locations of many of my clients. Complete comprehension hit me. He wanted to buy my company to save himself millions.

I nodded my understanding, and paused for a full minute to let my brain process the next step. I had not foreseen this. It made the offer a completely different animal.

He waited, although not quite patiently. He began, "Mrs. Denchek…"

I held my hand up to halt him. "I can see why you would want to purchase. What are you offering?"

He signaled to his man on the right again who came forward immediately, opening the briefcase on my desk. He pulled out a proposal. and placed it in front of me. The assistant closed the briefcase and went back to his corner.

I looked at the one page proposal and it took a great deal of control to not let Mr. Lobell see my shock. He was offering me $5 million dollars!

I read the page twice before I looked up. "I will have some clauses that need to be added and I want $6 million, plus additional bonuses for my current team, and an appropriate severance package if you decide to not keep any of them."

Mr. Lobell stood. I stood to receive his hand. He motioned to the man on the left this time, who came forward and opened his brief case, turned it toward me and left it on the desk as he moved back to his corner. "Mrs. Denchek, please accept this as payment for your time, as we work out the contractual detail of the purchase. If we come to a cross-roads that we cannot breach you are not obligated to repay this in any way. I am sure we can accommodate most any requests you have. I will have Rachel call to schedule a time for negotiations to begin."

With that he left, followed by his two men.

Oh my god! I am selling my business. For a ridiculous amount of money!

Chapter 11

Matthew came to sit next to me on the couch to begin our 'this is when we watch a movie time.'

"Matthew," I said. "I am going on an away contract again."

"What? I thought you weren't doing those anymore." The whine in his voice made me cringe.

"Well, Trevor's wife is having her baby any time now, so I can't rightly ask him to leave for a month. Shelly would never forgive me. So I told him I would go in his place."

"Damn!" He said with feigned emphasis, more like he was expected to say it, so he did his duty. "When do you leave?"

"Day after tomorrow. It's only a 30-day contract, so it won't be that big of a deal."

"Whoa. Way to give a guy heads up." He seemed earnestly unhappy about that part.

I smiled and chided with him playfully, "I'm sure you can handle living like a bachelor again for 30 days. You can have all the guys over every night if you want…to keep you company." I gave him a grandmotherly pinch to his cheek.

He perked up at the suggestion.

"Who knows, maybe I will find us another threesome while I'm there." I watched his reaction carefully.

Eye's widening and his attitude changed completely, "Oh, hell yeah! Glad you are the brains of this operation. Wait! You don't have any girls on the team right now, where are you gonna find her?"

"I don't know Matthew! I wasn't planning on doing a team member last time." With that I stalked out of the room.

I know he liked the idea of having another threesome, it was pretty much all he could talk about if we were on the subject of sex. It just pissed me off that it took the mention of another person to get him excited any more. Plus, he

had just called our relationship an operation…
exactly how I felt about it too I guess.

Two days didn't take much to fly by since
I didn't have anything packed or prepared. I
attempted to make the house ready for my
absence although I conceded a bitterness at feeling like it was my responsibility to take care of
him, even while I was away. I was very happy
now. The shuttle van I hired to pick us all up had
just arrived.

I said my goodbyes to Matthew quickly
with just a peck on the cheek, jumped into the
van next to Jeremy and we were off to the airport. Germany this time. I loved Germany. I had
a surprise for the rest of the team too. We were
not going to stay in some tiny little apartment for
four weeks, I had rented us rooms in an authentic
castle on a hill.

The flight was uneventful. Another shuttle van was waiting for us so we didn't need to
worry about getting train passes. When the van
merged into the chaotic traffic that was Europe,
Sam asked from the back, "Terry, where are we

staying? My wife wasn't too happy at not having an address."

I laughed, "Why? Did she think I was kidnapping you?" They all laughed. "Kidnapping you and putting a whole lot of money in your bank account that is." They laughed some more. "Don't worry guys, I actually took the liberty of letting each of your significant others know the address and a phone they could leave a message on if they needed to get in touch with us." I had neglected to do this for my own significant other though.

"Is it some secret mission this time Big T?" Rick asked.

I turned from the front seat to look back at my team. I admired each and every one of them. The knowledge that this was our last contract together saddened me. It was something they didn't know yet. When we got back to the States they would work for a big conglomerate. How could I refuse what they had offered?

Some, if not all of the team would be able to stay on. I was sure they would keep Jeremy. He was young, had a newer education, and might be open to a lower wage, if they asked. The other guys might have to make some hard choices. They would have to learn to take orders most likely. I was sure they would not have a boss like me in charge.

Not that I didn't give orders, I had learned

from Ashley how to get people to do what I wanted, while having them think it was their idea. It made for very happy employees.

One of the conditions to the buyout was a raise in bonus on this last contract, the more expensive hotel, VIP treatment, and that I would have another three months after the contract to let the team know and give them all time to find somewhere to land if they decided not to stay on. It was the best deal I could have worked out for the team.

For me, on the other hand, I had it good. I had already invested the pre-downpayment in a private securities fund that was only in my name. I didn't know why I had done it that way at first, now I knew though. I could admit to myself finally, the end of this company for me was probably the end of the business of my husband as well.

To the guys I said in a dramatic, serious voice, "Gentlemen, do you accept the mission?"

Rick started humming the Mission Impossible theme song, and the guys all laughed.

Jeremy said softly, "Seriously ma'am, where are we going?"

The rest of the guys all loudly chimed in together, "Whoa boy! No! Don't call her that."

I smiled and corrected him gently, "That will be the last time you ever call me that, unless you want me to tie you up and get a whip." I said sarcastically. I had meant it as a joke, although I saw a brief glint of excitement in his eyes when I said it. He immediately hid it and went back to the shy quiet man I had hired. I brushed it off without a thought.

The guys all started asking at once for the real story of what was going on.

"Ok, ok. I'll give. I wanted to surprise you because it is something special. Since it is only a 30-day contract and I haven't been on one in years, I decided to splurge a bit."

"Right on!" Ken said. "We're staying at the Ritz guys!"

Hoots and hollers, whistles and smiles, the van rocked its way closer to our accommodations with glee. If I could let them keep this up just little longer, I could see their faces of amazement when we actually started up the driveway.

We made our way onto the road that followed the Rhine, and the guys calmed with the beautiful views. The cab driver caught the jovial nature, and began telling us about all the areas we were passing and what each side road lead to.

"Many vineries." he pronounced it like a V instead of a W with his accent.

To this, everyone was cheering again, the driver was happy to be welcomed into the conversation.

Rick asked the driver, "Hey, you can tell us where we are going, right buddy?"

The driver winked at me and shouted with a fist to the air, "Ve go up da Rhine!"

The guys sent out boos and hisses, then they all laughed.

"This is pretty far if we are working in Frankfurt, don't you think ma'. Um..Terry?" Jeremy said.

I was still laughing from the last round. I calmed down to answer him. "It is only a 20 minute drive from where we are staying to our work location. I don't know about you Jeremy, but I drive twice that far in the States to get to work." He nodded in agreement.

Just then the driver said, "Willkommen! To Hotel Berg Liebenstien!" He pulled onto a small road that lead away from the river. The hotel was still out of sight though. We made our way through the woods, and began ascending a fairly steep incline.

The guys were all looking out the windows trying to see anything other than trees. Winding our way up the drive, the trees opened enough on one side and allowed us to see the Rhine again, from a much higher vantage point this time.

"Wow." said Sam. "We are definitely going to have some great pictures to take home. This is beautiful Terry."

Just then, the tree line stopped, and we drove into a large circular driveway and pulled up to the castle's front entrance.

"No way Terry!" Rick said with excitement. Everyone was impressed. As they piled out of the van, they all stared up in amazement at the towers and turrets. Steve slowly turned around, taking a panoramic image in his digital mind. Rick and Sam were my two jovial kids. Rick actually was bouncing like a kid with the anticipation of staying in such an amazing place. I smiled, mentally patting myself on the back. I did good.

I turned back to the driver who had finished putting our luggage out. He said, "Vat time in der morning?"

"Um acht Uhr, danka." I said in German and paid him. He nodded, got back in the van, and drove away.

Chapter 12

Our time on the Rhine was absolutely amazing. Everyone on the team was anxious to get back to the Berg at the end of each day as the host always had something new to offer us. We had a campfire cookout in the backwoods one day, horseback riding on another, a chartered boat ride on the Rhine the next, and many chartered bus rides to go visit some of the other castles.

We visited at least 5 wineries while we were there. Each gave us bottles of fabulous wines ,which we shipped home by the case. My own favorite wine was made here outside of Frankfurt, and they had just one case left of the very expensive Vise. Only grapes upon the first frost could be used to make it, so there was always a limited supply, which of course drove the price through the roof.

I hadn't expected to spend so much time with my team. We worked all day together, then we played all evening together. Jeremy became very much a solid part of the team and a silent connection was building between him and me. The entire experience was so good for morale. Jeremy became the sounding block for everyone else's woes about their spouses, since he didn't have one. We didn't really expect him to tell us what to do about it, he was young, we just needed to vent.

When I started the contract I had planned on calling Matthew every night, just like when I was in Japan. The first week though, I missed calling him on Saturday because we had all gotten extremely drunk at the winery. When we made it home, I was lucky to manage to make it to my bed, let alone call Matthew.

Sunday evening was not a great phone call. I knew it wouldn't be. It was the first time I had ever missed a call while away, the first telltale sign. I decided I would get it done with as soon as we got back.

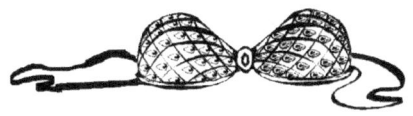

Matthew wasn't too happy at the missed call, I could tell immediately, although he brushed it off saying, "Well, I went out with the boys anyway. You didn't call by 10 so I figured you weren't going to."

"Oh, that's cool. You guys have a good time?" I asked, seriously interested.

"Yes. We went to a titty bar. I spent a lot of money. Those girls are hot and I asked two of them about coming home to meet you. I think they played me."

I smirked to myself. "Really?" How could he possibly think a stripper was going to go home with him? That is what they are paid to do, to make you feel like you are the one, yet when it comes down to it, they are just there for a pay-check, just like everyone else.

He was down on himself. "Yeah. I know it was stupid of me to think it. So! Did you find any hotties yet?"

Oh god, I thought. "No. We went to a winery, the team and I. They have you taste everything, and by the time we left, I could barely walk. Sorry. That's why I missed my call last night."

He was disappointed. "Oh. Well, get on it girl." he tried to sound encouraging. "We got another threesome coming, right?"

"Yeah, sure. Hey, I'm gonna run. The host of the hotel has dinner waiting for us."

"Oh, ok…sure. I'll talk to you tomorrow right?"

"Yep. Love ya."

"I love you too. Bye." We hung up.

Wow. Matthew never says 'I love you' all proper like that. He must feel it too, the end. I took a quick inhale. I hadn't admitted that fully to myself, until now.

Everyone was sitting around the large dining table. The food smelled amazing, as always.

"Hey! There she is." Rick said.

"Now we can eat." Jeremy chimed in. Cheers went around the room.

I said, "Sorry guys. Danke Herr Eckehardt. The spouse phone call ya know."

I brought gloom into the room with me, and the guys felt it. I got an "awe" along with a pat on the back when I sat down.

"Let's eat!" I attempted joviality.

Everyone began filling thier plates. Jeremy leaned over and said softly, "Everything alright on the home front?"

"Yeah, sure." My mood soured. I said, "You know men, they always want what they don't have."

"What is that supposed to mean?" he prodded.

"Awe, nothing. It's not a conversation for.. Ah…mixed company." I glanced around the table, luckily, no one else seemed to be tuned in to Jeremy and me.

"Ok." he said, "We can adjourn to the library for coffee after dinner, just you and me."

"That's ok. I'll be fine."

"No, no. It's no biggie. I took sociology as a minor, I love this stuff. It's kinda making me think I'm in the wrong profession. I'm a good listener, I don't interject my own opinions too much, and I would never tell…just like a doctor's oath." he crossed his heart with a scouts two finger pledge.

I smiled, reminiscing on what happened the last time I told someone about what Matthew was asking of me. I did not think he would be ok with me 'testing waters' with this one though, that just wouldn't be on the docket. I thought it would be nice to chat with someone about it though, and as long as I didn't drink any alcohol, I would be fine keeping my hands to myself.

I shrugged my shoulders and said, "Sure… maybe."

"Ok, whatever you need."

We both went back to eating. Jeremy joined the conversation of the table, soon laughter could be heard again. It lightened my mood.

Herr Eckehardt, passed around a bottle of Vise. One of the guys had let slip that it was my favorite. I couldn't refuse, although I restrained myself to just one glass.

Our host asked, "Vould anyone like zome coffee?" This was typical after dinner. Steve and Sam both said their thank yous, but no, they were off to their spouse calls. The rest of us said yes.

We all helped clear the plates, and put the dining room back to order. Rick and Ken took charge of getting the dishes done while Eckehardt made coffee, and passed it about. Once I had mine, I slowly made my way to the library.

Jeremy saw my direction and followed. We walked through the halls, admiring the suits of armor and the huge wooden beams in the ceiling. This place was beautiful, I wished I could live in a castle permanently.

Jeremy shut the library door behind us, turning the key, locking us in. I gave him a questioning glance at this action. I thought it was probably a good idea. I wouldn't want someone walking in on the conversation we were about to have.

Jeremy started with a bit of humor. He gestured to the couch, lengthwise to indicate what I should be doing, then cleared his throat and mocked a pad of paper with a pen. "Now, what seems to be the problem?"

I smiled. Out with it, I thought. No reason

to hold back this time. I reclined back onto the couch and let loose. "My husband wants to have another threesome, and he expects me to find this person while I am here in Germany to bring home with me."

His eye widened. He sat in stunned silence.

I continued, "I know. It's a lot to take in. You probably never would have thought I had already had one to begin with and here I am talking about having another. Long story short, I was on a contract in Japan, and basically fell in love with this…ah…woman. She taught me how to be with a woman, and then I told my husband. He had always wanted a threesome so badly; he flew there, and we had one.

It actually made our sex life amazing…for a while, that is. I guess just like our marriage, the glitter wears off after a while.

So, we are back to him constantly nagging me about finding another woman, and me getting pissed off because he needs another woman."

We sat in silence as I let the information sink in. He started to nod his head in understanding. He was good at listening.

"He went hunting at a strip club last night, and was sorely disappointed that I haven't been looking myself. He actually ordered me to 'get to it." I indicated finger quotes in the air.

"I see." Jeremy said. "Let me understand something real quick. You had one, your sex life was great afterward, now it's not so much, he's asking for another, and….you don't want one this time?"

I got defensive, "I don't know. I just would like him to want just me for a change. Our entire sex life revolves around that threesome and now, about finding another woman to do it again." I sank back on the couch. I could totally see where he was leading.

He held up his hands, "Ok, ok. I just was getting everything clear in my head. Can I ask one other thing?" I nodded. "Have you ever thought about having a threesome with another man?"

This time it was my turn to be silenced. I had never thought about it. He was right though, why is it that we were only looking for another woman? What about me? He got to have his fantasy of two women, wasn't it my turn to have two men? Not that I had ever fantasized about that, but now that I was thinking about it…I could definitely see some perks to the idea. I remembered how erotic it had been, I thought about Ashley's wide tongue jabbing into my mouth like a penis while Matthew fucked me. I could be seriously turned on just by thinking about that.

Stop it! I chastised myself. I sat up to right myself, and my mind. Don't get yourself all worked up right now while you are sitting here, all good girl, talking to a team member.

Jeremy stood up, and said down to me, "I think I will retire for the night. I believe I have said enough for one evening."

"Thank you Jeremy. Yes, you said the perfect thing actually. Maybe you are in the wrong profession." I stood, gave him a peck on the cheek, and we both went to our separate rooms.

Chapter 13

That night as I lay in my bed going over the conversation, flashes of another man kept entering the picture of my marriage bed. I had to keep turning off the pictures because it was always Jeremy's face. Finally, I resigned to change the subject in my head and think of something less erotic or I knew I would never get to sleep.

I woke with a gasp and reached between my legs to find my panties drenched. My dreams were so vivid. I had just climaxed. I lay there going back over the dream. Sensual, hot bodies, full of muscles and sweat. Me sucking an unfamiliar cock, while being fucked from behind. Positions changed to me on top, riding Matthew…and there he was again, Jeremy.

He had made his way into my dream. I dreamed of stroking his cock in my hand, and it was so close to Matthew's face that I directed it there with purpose. "Please Matthew," I pleaded. "I want to see you suck it. Do it for me."

He opened his mouth slightly and dabbed his tongue to the end of Jeremy's cock. I pulled it closer and he allowed it to penetrate his mouth, wrapping his lips around it. Jeremy's quick inhale, and quivering exhale made me cum… that had been the moment I woke.

"Wow!" I said out loud to myself. "That is a definite yes in the argument of the power of suggestion."

I couldn't believe how erotic that was to me, watching another man stick his cock into my husband's mouth. I couldn't imagine him agreeing to it, although my mind was screaming that it would definitely be nice if he would. I really wanted to experience that.

I smiled as I went through the dream over, and over, while I was dressing for the day. By the time I made it to my make-up, I decided I needed to start trying to get it out of my mind or I was not going to be able to work. Sitting next to Jeremy could lead to an issue for me as well.

I paused to wonder if his cock really looked

like that… "Stop that!" I finished my make-up and laid back down on my bed. I needed to give myself another orgasm before this day began, or I would have to pull Jeremy aside and break my vows.

I caught Jeremy watching me after lunch. It was just a tiny, split second I saw it, and I knew he knew I had given a lot of thought to his question, and he was wondering what happened. At dinner that night, I sat on the opposite side from him, I declined coffee for the evening, going straight to my room.

Again, I needed to distract myself from the obvious thought lines, so I could get to sleep. I went back to my faithful visions of Ashley to give myself an orgasm, hoping that it would wear me out, and that I would fall asleep without thinking of what it would be like…

I slid my hand down his pants and grasped a hot, throbbing penis. Slowly sliding my hand up and down its satin shaft. Matthew kissed my neck from behind, and I leaned my head back on his shoulder as his finger spread the lips of my pussy. His cock was hard against my back and his hips undulated to stroke it against me.

I looked up into Jeremy's eyes and he came down to kiss me. Sliding his tongue gently along my lower lip. Matthew joined us, his lips coming to us. I pulled back slightly so I could watch the two of them… I awoke.

My hand was already between my legs this time, a finger half inserting into me, my juices everywhere. My body shook with the climax. I giggled at the thought of what was making them happen. How is this so erotic to me? Just because it is forbidden? Something people say isn't right?

Whatever. How can it be acceptable for a woman-woman-man threesome, and then not for a man-man-woman threesome? Apparently, it was just as erotic, maybe even more so in my mind. I need to do something about this.

That evening, during my call to Matthew, I decided to go for it. "Matthew," I said. "Why do you always ask me if I found a woman for us?"

"Well, because you are good at it I guess. I can't say I have tried that much, but whenever I bring up the fact that I have a wife, they leave. They don't even let me get as far as letting them know you are ok with it."

I laughed sincerely. I could see how that would be a problem. I moved closer to the subject. "I actually was referring to the woman part. Why don't you go find us a man to have one with?"

"What! No way! I'm not doin' some dude."

With more force than I had intended, "Fine. You get whatever you want, and I have to do everything to get it for you. Some day you will think better of it." I hung up the phone.

I had no idea what he thought about what had just happened. I had never been so brash with him. Maybe, the power of suggestion would work on him as well. Besides, it was true. He got to have his three-some and even though I have already admitted to myself that he would never go for it, it pisses me off that he won't even consider it.

I got up from the phone cubby, and started toward my room. Jeremy was nervously waiting there. He must have heard it. How am I going to handle this?

"Um… Hi Terry. I didn't mean to be here… now. I mean, I didn't mean to over hear what just happened." He was very nervous about what might happen next.

I smiled. "There's nothing to apologize for, Jeremy. We all have our spouse call woes. This one may be more awkward due to our conversation," I gestured to him and I. "I agree, though… here, come in my room so we can talk. I don't want to have this conversation out here in the hallway."

He followed me in, and I looked both ways down the hall to see if anyone had seen or heard before I shut and locked the door. He gave me an identical look of questioning, to the one I had given him, just two days before. I shrugged my shoulders.

I looked down at the floor in contemplation.

"Terry, it's ok if you don't want to talk about it. Men have a much more difficult time accepting that sex with another man is ok, and that it doesn't necessarily make them gay."

"No. That is not what I wanted to tell you."

"Oh. What is it?"

"I ah…. I have been having dreams about… Well… you know. You suggested something and so my mind put a scenario together and ah… Well, I keep waking up after just having climaxed, in my dreams."

"Wow. That must be one great fantasy," he said with a smile on his face.

"I didn't expect it to be that erotic to me. When I saw him take your cock in his mouth, it was like totally overwhelming!"

"Wait. What?"

"What?" I had gotten so wrapped up in telling him what was happening to me, I was taken aback that he was making me pause.

He said slowly, "You said when he took *my* cock," he pointed to himself.

"Oh shit. Ahhhh…yes. About that. That was part of what I wanted to talk to you about." My face was blushing, I could feel the heat building.

I had so just totally stuck my foot in my mouth.

He took one step and suddenly had me in his arms, holding the back of my head, he plunged his tongue into my mouth. Pure ecstasy shot through my body. The tingle of the first kiss engulfed me, and I wrapped my arms around him, reciprocating the passion.

He was so tall. His hips were thrusting forward and the heat from his pants was warm against my belly as I felt his pleasure swell.

"Please," I whispered, "please don't tell anyone."

"No. I won't. I have wanted this ever since I laid eyes on you Terry. Please let me fuck you." He pleaded with me, in a deep husky whisper, between kisses on my mouth and kisses on my neck. His hands were everywhere, grabbing my tits, massaging my butt, gently pulling my hair to give my head a better angle for his kisses.

My breathing was beyond excited, I'm sure he knew it. "Yes. Yes, fuck me. Oh my god I have been dreaming of your cock inside me. In my mouth, in my pussy."

He whipped me up, into his arms and brought me gently to the bed where he immediately took off my clothes. "Oh Terry. You are so fucking hot. He dove for my breast and sucked it hard.

As he sucked my other nipple, he maneuvered to get his clothes off. I pushed him back and sat up in excitement to see his cock. Will it be like my dream?

He stood and his pants dropped to his ankles. It wasn't anything like I had imagined it. My dream had made him long, thinner than Matthew, and very pink. I don't know why I dreamt it that way. His cock was spectacular! Even better than I dreamed.

I grabbed it in both hands, and slammed my mouth down around it. I could barely get it in, he was so thick. It was much darker, and he was uncircumcised. His cock was so full, and throbbing, there wasn't much skin left to cover his gorgeous mushroom head. I forced my mouth open as wide as I could, I wanted to get as much in as possible.

He sucked air in and watched me engorge myself on his beautiful penis. I moaned with the erotic pleasure of having it in my mouth finally. What would it be like to be spread that far open, I wondered. I used both hands to stroke him, then I plunged my mouth on him, over, and over. I felt I couldn't get enough. I wanted more.

I grabbed his hand and put it on the back of my head, encouraging him to push me further. I wanted it all. He pushed gently, and I gagged. It sent my juices flooding out, making a wet spot on the bed.

I paused to let my throat relax. "Oh my god, that is so fucking hot. Your cock is gorgeous." I looked up into his eyes as I stroked him with my hands.

"Terry. You don't have to suck it that far. I know its big, not many people can get it that far in their mouth."

"No. I love it. I *want* to gag on it. You should feel how wet my pussy is now. Please, push my head a little bit more. I want it down my throat." And with that, I jammed my mouth around him again.

He took my head with both hands this time, pushing harder. "Oh man. Oh yes. Terry, you're a fucking rockin' cock sucker. Oh my god, Oh yes." His breathing became erratic as I continued to force him down my throat, twisting my head back and forth sucking and pulling. Even though I was thoroughly enjoying the head of him slamming down the back of my throat, I did not want him to cum yet.

I took a deep breath and gave one last shove, gagging hard, I grabbed his ass with both hands so I could hold myself to him as long as possible. I wanted to release the slickness that happens in my throat when I gag, and when I finally pulled back I used my tongue to rub it around his head gently.

"Oh man, Terry. That was the best head I have ever had. I don't usually get that close to cumming from a BJ."

"Well, I didn't want you to cum yet. I think I

could suck that cock until you screamed! I want you to fuck my pussy, spread me open with that big thing."

He came down upon me quickly. I laid back and spread my legs. He laid on me fully and put his hand between our legs. His fingers found my lips and he gently swirled his finger around the outside and then quickly dipped it in.

"Oh, you're right, you are dripping wet." He grabbed his cock and guided it to me.

When he was sure it was aimed correctly he began to push, gently at first. I could feel his head was wet with my saliva and it slid easily inside with the 'pop' I love so much. This time though, it was so much more. His girth was stretching me. I moaned.

He pushed some more and was filling me to the edge of pain. He continued pushing, my moans indicating it was good.

"Jeremy, oh god, you're fucking me."

"Yes." He pushed harder and harder. "Your pussy is so tight. Oh fuck Terry." I could feel the hair at the base tickling me, his balls resting against my ass. I wanted more.

"Jeremy, fuck me. Give it all to me. Plunge it deep." I spread my legs further so he could go deeper. Opening my pussy to his swelling.

He pounded it in, and I had to suppress a scream of ecstasy as I came. He slowed slightly, yet continued a steady pace until I could breathe again. I whispered, "Yes, oh my god, yes. That cock feels so good. Do it! Do it again and again. My dream didn't compare to this. It feels so good." My body shivered with pleasure as he slowly dipped his shaft in and out, letting me feel every inch with the intensity of the orgasm that had just passed.

"Jesus Terry. I can't believe I'm fucking you. I'm going to explode next time you cum. Your pussy clenched down so tight just then, I can't believe I didn't go over already."

"Please don't cum early. I want to do this for a while."

"Don't worry. I want to feel your tight pussy too. It feels so good. Soft, silky, wet." He lay down on me and continued his naughty whispers in my ear. "You're so wet."

I whimpered, "Yes. I want more." I raised my legs and encircled his back.

He kissed me, our tongues' dance deep and full. He increased his rhythm and began to slam deeper inside me.

"Yes Jeremy. That's it. Fuck that big cock inside me."

He did. Over and over he slammed his pelvis against me, sending his giant, throbbing cock deep inside me. I felt like it was getting even bigger than when I had my mouth wrapped around it. I could fuck this cock for hours. Please don't stop.

He propped himself up, grabbing one of my legs, lifting it up next to my face. "Oh. Fuck yes. Oh Terry, your pussy is so fucking sweet." He watched his cock slide in and out of my pussy. "Oh god. Your lips are pulling and sucking it.

He slammed it deep, over and over, slapping the skin, faster and faster. The pleasure of such a large cock was sending me into multiple orgasms. My body was limp with pleasure.

He dug his hands under my butt, and lay his chest against mine. Grinding his hips into mine, rubbing my clit, again, and again, and again that giant cock pushed deeper, bashing all the right places with his head.

He would pull it all the way out, then let me feel it pop back in slowly, just the head at first, and then, slam it all the way down. It took forever, and just a split second before he was doing it again. Every centimeter was vibrating my vagina. My lips were pulling at his foreskin, in and out, in and out. The teasing was driving me insane, causing orgasm on top of orgasm.

"Oh god. Terry. I'm gonna cum." His body was shivering all over and I felt his cock swell even further. I could tell it would only be moments before I would have another myself.

"Yes! Slam it hard then. Fucking jam it down so deep and make me cum again, cum with me! Oh!"

He increased his speed to a crazy level,

then it was like he lost control of his body and it became sporadic and ended quivering. He shook for quite some time before his body relaxed. Mine was so relaxed, I doubted I could even stand at the moment. The feelings of complete satisfaction I had with Ashley were flooding back. It felt so good. I know almost everyone would see it as wrong.

Maybe that was why my marriage was failing. Maybe I wasn't meant to be with only one person. My body craved other things, other people, this euphoric feeling. I did not ever remember having this with Matthew. How could I tell him this time? He wouldn't understand. Maybe I didn't want him to understand.

"Hey."

I hadn't noticed Jeremy recover and turn to look at me. "Hey yourself," I said in return, and turned to smile at him.

"You were a million miles away just then. I would have thought you would have stuck around at least till I could get dressed and leave the room." he chided playfully.

"I'm sorry. That was truly fantastic. I got this overwhelming, euphoric, feeling, and I guess my mind just wandered off."

"So this happens all the time?"

"Absolutely not. I've only been with one other person that it happened with before."

"Your husband?"

"Ah…unfortunately, no. It was with the woman I told you about. I don't know. Maybe I only let loose when it's something I'm not supposed to be doing." I giggled lightly.

"No. I can see that. It makes the eroticism heightened to be a no-no. I am glad to hear I am one of the few who made it happen for you. I was worried you were thinking about your husband again."

"I was. We are done, me and my husband. I have barely admitted it to myself, let alone told anyone yet, even him."

"Wow. Why? If you can get him to have another person with you guys it would probably be good again, for at least a while longer."

"I suppose. I want to have you though and I am sure he won't even consider a guy. He will only want a woman and I'm not up to being the one who must facilitate it all. I think I'm just not meant to be married. I think I should be single so I can fuck whoever I want, when I want."

He gently brushed the hair off my face. "I think that will get lonely eventually. We all want to share our lives and that means you continue to share with one person; otherwise you only have a few things you can reminisce about with each other."

"Hmmm… I didn't think of it like that. Well, I want someone who will have sex with anyone then, male or female, hell…I don't know…

maybe even more than one at a time, an orgy."

"So, go hang out at swinger events. You will find lots of people who like to have sex with… lots of people." He winked at me, and got up to get dressed.

I propped myself up on one elbow. "Don't go. Stay here till later."

"No ma'am, I don't believe that would be prudent at this point." He continued to put his pants on.

"Oh, wham, bam, thank you ma'am and you're outta there. Huh?"

"Absolutely not. I would love to stay. I would love to fuck you in the morning, and every day until we leave. I just think the other team members might see you in a different light if they knew and I don't want that to happen." He put his shirt on and sat on the side of the bed.

"Yes, you're right." They will think the worst of me soon enough, I thought to myself.

He leaned over to kiss me. "We only have six days left anyway. I don't know about you, but I think I can wait six whole days till we fuck again. It will make it more exhilarating to wait. And who knows, maybe you will find a way to get that three-some arranged. If not, I would rather we wait until you have told him you were leaving at least. I don't want to put any pressure there. I don't want to get caught in the middle of something either. I love what just happened and can't wait till we can do it again." He quickly kissed me, and swiftly left the room.

I wasn't given a chance to say anything back. He was right. I didn't need that looming over me with the team, when I was about to tell them about the sellout. I also didn't want Matthew to find out. I wasn't very good at keeping secrets, mostly because I didn't like them. I was however, going to keep this one for now. Man! I really wanted to fuck him again, right now.

I flung myself back onto the bed and recalled the evening as I fell into a heavy, wonderful sleep.

Chapter 14

There were a few awkward moments over the next week, where I was sexually anxious in mixed company with Jeremy. I had to forcefully make myself not look at him, smile at him, brush up against him. I took on an almost pissed off at him attitude, although after day two, I thought better of that as some of my teammates might figure out that was what I was doing; a reverse psychology thing.

I kept to myself more, trying to stay away from him. I spoke with Matthew more, although it was mostly quibbling about our sex life. I couldn't find anything that even made him think about the option of a man. I told him I wouldn't call him the last two days. I wanted to make sure to take the guys into Frankfurt before we left.

I did show them the town. We finished our job three days early, which we always tried to do. Over deliver, and bring it in faster than expected, that was our motto. Typically, we would re-book our flights early and go home, but I had promised some extras, and since this trip had been a highlight already, they all agreed to go with it.

The trip home was uneventful. I sent word to everyone's spouses of our arrival time so they could all meet at the airport. Again, I neglected this information for Matthew.

Instead, I made up a lie about how he couldn't make it, and had a car arranged to take me and Jeremy home. Jeremy didn't know anything about it so it was truly a surprise to him, making it seem casual.

Once we were in the car, and on our way, I said, "I'm going to stop at the store and pick up some drinks. I would like you to come over to have some drinks with us, let Matthew get to know you. I think it might be easier if he met someone who was open."

He smiled. "It might work. I'm not sure though, I might be uncomfortable."

"No. Just erase what happened between us in your mind. What would you act like if we were just three people? You're a friend of mine, and I want us all to hang out, that's it."

"Ok. If that is the way you want to play it. I don't know if it will go anywhere though. Have you been talking to him about it?"

"Not much. He gets pissy when I do. If it comes up, it comes up. If not...I will talk to him more about it after you are gone. No worries."

We chatted about all the great things we had seen and done in Germany, and when we arrived at my house, we were full-on laughing about the waiter in a restaurant we had been to in Frankfurt.

I opened the door and walked into a mess of a house. Matthew was on the couch in his underwear. There were beer cans everywhere, and two pizza boxes. The air smelled dank.

"Well hello there dear." I said. "I see you haven't done much while I was gone."

"Whoa!" he said as he jumped up. "I wasn't expecting you...and uh....a guest. Shit! Let me go put some clothes on." He jogged past us to the bedroom.

Jeremy said, "Hey man! No worries. I'm sure you don't have anything I haven't seen before. That's what my mom always said when she walked in on me." He laughed, and we made our way into the kitchen to deposit the groceries I had bought.

Matthew called out from the bedroom, "True dat man. You're Jeremy, right?" He came out buttoning his shorts. "The new guy?"

Jeremy held his hand out. "Yep, dat's me. How'd ya know? What gave it away?"

"Only because I've never met you. I know the rest of the team." they shook hands and Matthew gave me a peck on the cheek. "Hey babe, bring me anything special from Germany?"

"Only wine. Everything else is from the local store here." I laughed as I showed him the beer and liquor I brought home for the evening. "I figured you hadn't been shopping in a while, so I did enough to get us through till I can get back to the store."

"You're the best babe, you really know me," he said at full volume for Jeremy's ears. Then in a half whisper he said, "But what about the special present I asked you to bring me? Did you find it?" He hugged me, and pretended to be mushy with me.

Jeremy came around the corner from the living room, "What's the special present?"

I quickly piped up to Jeremy and said, "Oh, ah… Nothing." To Matthew I said, in his ear loud enough that I was pretty sure Jeremy would hear as well, "Babe knock it off unless you want me to ask Jeremy to be your special present. We can talk about it later." I saw Jeremy quickly hide a smile, and knew he was aware of what I had just done.

"Ow!" He said and spun away from me

and grabbed a beer. To Jeremy he asked, "You stayin' for a beer man? Or just helping in with the groceries?"

Jeremy looked at me, and I said, "Yes, stay for one at least right?"

"Sure. I'll take one man."

Matthew threw him a can and they both popped tops and took a drink. I continued to unload the groceries, and randomly picked up empties as I came upon them.

"Hey man, come sit down. I'm sure I can find a spot I didn't spill any beer on. What did you guys do for fun over there?" He and Jeremy went into the living room. Matthew picked up a few cans, and brought them to the trash, to at least somewhat help with cleaning up the mess he had made.

"Oh man! It was great! I've only been on a one-weeker since being with the company, and it was only to Cali. This was my first to another country, and what a country! Did you know we stayed in a castle?" He fell right into chattering in a way that was built for Matthew's intelligence.

"What? No way! Babe! What's up with that? You guys have pictures?"

"Oh, totally," Jeremy said. "We have so many pictures its crazy. We visited like 50 castles, and probably double that on the wineries and beer makers."

"So you guys were totally sloshed the whole

time you were there?" He chided with a big smile. He was enjoying the conversation.

I finished in the kitchen and made my way to the couch. I had to make three trips back to the trash with empties and pizza boxes before I could sit finally down. Before I actually did I asked, "So, do I need to put a towel down on the couch before I sit? Did you really spill beer?"

"No, babe. I didn't. I don't think…" He laughed in Jeremy's direction.

"So how did you guys get any work done if you did all this other stuff…and you know… getting drunk every day?"

I said, "We didn't get drunk every day. I think in total it was only about four or five days we went drinking. We did try to visit somewhere every day after work. That is how we got to see so much. Then, like always, we finished early so I took everyone to Frankfurt for the last two days."

"Whoa! Everyone? Damn! That sounds like the best trip you've ever been on. I shoulda come out for that one." He got up to get another beer. "You ready for another one Jer? What about you babe?"

"Ah… sure." Jeremy looked at his beer, then me. Shrugged his shoulders and downed his mostly full beer.

"Nope. I just got mine babe. You are racing ahead. Just feels great to not be on a plane any more, or in a car, or in an airport." Jeremy and I both laughed at that.

Jeremy questioned toward Matthew, "You ever been there man? To Germany I mean?"

"Naw. I don't travel much. I did take one trip a few years back to Japan." He flung himself onto the couch, then nudged me with an elbow and a wink, "to visit my wife for Christmas. Now that was fun! I know whatcha mean though. That plane ride was forever and a day."

"Germany isn't quite that far, it just feels that way." I said, trying to be ok with his ignorance.

Jeremy turned the conversation back to Japan. "You must have really enjoyed Japan. That has got to be the trip of a life time."

Matthew sat upright, "You're tellin' me. I had so much fucking fun there, I can't even begin to tell ya." He glanced my way. I smiled and nodded back to him.

I wanted him to feel he could speak freely with Jeremy, so I said, "I'm going to go change out of these clothes and order a pizza. I hope you aren't tired of pizza. We haven't had any in a month, and I don't want to cook."

Matthew was fine with it. "Sure babe. Get comfy. I'm fine with pizza, you know me." He got up with me, and headed to the kitchen. "You want another beer man?"

I went into my bedroom, closing the door behind me. I got out some comfy, yet slightly risqué, shorts and a t-shirt, and headed into the bathroom. I took a long hot shower, giving them plenty of time to chat 'man-to-man'. I was pretty sure Jeremy could lead Matthew in the right direction. My pussy was pulsing slightly with arousing thoughts of what might be about to happen.

I wished I could hear their conversation. How would Jeremy ask him? Direct and to the point, like he did with me? I don't think that would work with Matthew, he'd put his 'gay-guard' up so fast, even I wouldn't be able to bring it down.

How would Matthew respond? Would he wonder if this has been set up the whole time? Would he think I have already had sex with Jeremy? Man, I hope he doesn't. That would probably put up a wall too.

Damn it! I want to know what they are saying! Is it going to happen, or not? My mind was racing as I slowly, methodically, prepared myself for an evening of pleasure.

I shaved everywhere. I powdered and lotioned all the right places. I put on some-makeup, not too much, just enough to accent the important features. A light spitz of perfume, and I was ready.

The steam of the shower followed me into the bedroom. Matthew came in as I was drying my hair. "You are one hot piece of ass babe."

I smiled. "Thanks babe." Even though it was a rough manly way to say it, he really did like the way I looked.

"So, babe." He said, more hesitant than he should have. "Your boy… is he…gay?"

"What? No! … I don't think so." I added for good measure.

"Yea, I don't think he is either, just wanted to check."

"Why? What have you two been talking about?" I pretended to be worried. "Is he gone?"

He rushed to reassure me, "No, he's still here. Nothing…not much, I mean. I kinda let slip maybe, just maybe…what my present had been in Japan." He cringed, expecting me to berate him with reprimanding words. I didn't, I simply raised one eyebrow as I continued drying my hair with the towel.

He continued, "I don't know. I remember you were pretty pissed at me that I wouldn't even consider a three-some with a guy…"

At this I snapped in a whisper, "What? Did you tell him we would do that with him? How could you? He works on my team!"

"No, no, no. I didn't, I promise! I didn't even imply that we were interested in something like that. That is why I came in here."

"What? So you could ask my permission first?" I threw the towel on the bed with drama, and walked back into the bathroom. I couldn't very well have him see my face. I couldn't control the smile. He had let slip one word. The word that let me know that this particular fantasy was probably about to happen. 'We' He said *we* were interested.

"It's not like that, babe. We just couldn't seem to get away from the conversation about Japan. It was like he kept wanting me to tell him all the details, and I knew you were gonna be pissed to find out I had even told him one thing, let alone the whole story. I had to get out of the room." He paused, exhaling a breath so loud I heard it in the bathroom.

I came back out to look at him. "What? Out with it. Some burning question is about to bore a hole through your brain if you don't let it come out."

"Well, plus, you said you wanted to have a three-some with a guy and…he's cool, I like him. I mean, not in that way of course."

"Of course."

"Well, I thought maybe you might want to do it with him. He seems pretty excited to talk about three-somes… And I thought maybe you could steer the conversation toward one with men, and we could feel him out, so to speak. You know, just to see if he was interested, or if he would freak out and think that I was gay or something."

I made my voice casual. "I don't know babe. It's that whole work thing."

Jeremy must be really good. Matthew was thinking this entire idea had come from himself, rather than Jeremy leading him into it.

"I know, I know."

"I mean, with Ashley, I didn't know how I was going to deal with it when we got back to the states, you know, how our friends might react once they found out, or how my co-workers would react. But, she solved that one by not even coming back, so…"

He whispered heavily, "I know, I know. That is why we have to feel him out first. See if he would even consider it. Then we can talk about how it would ruin your reputation at work. You know, let him know in certain words that it would have to be kept a secret." He looked at me expectantly.

I was really surprised to see him so excited about this. I couldn't imagine how the conversation was going to come around, I had never thought it would be him trying to work out the details and finessing me into the idea.

"Ok." I said. "This is how we are going to play this game."

He nodded like a little boy again, about to make a bargain for candy.

"You go back out there and first apologize for leaving him alone so long, that was rude."

"Oh, yes. I will tell him I was getting frisky with you, that will be fine. All guys understand that." He mentally took notes, and nodded his head.

I continued, "Go ahead, tell him more of the Japan story, ask him if he has ever had a three-some." He nodded again.

I quickly added, "Don't ask if it was with girls though. Maybe he will just tell us he's done it before, or something, you never know." I looked off into space as if I needed to think more about the details of how to work this. Matthew nodded agreement. He knew I was in the command position, and he knew how to take orders.

"If he doesn't let us know either way, ask him if he ever wanted to… Well, you are a guy, you should say it like you know he has; dot, dot, dot." I spoke the punctuation that implied to let him fill in the blanks.

"Oh, that's perfect babe. We will lead him around the conversation until he lets it slip in front of you. Yes." He brought a triumphant fist down in front of his face.

"I will be back in there by then. Make sure you abruptly stop the conversation when I come in, no matter where you are, so it looks like you weren't suppose to tell him any of this. I will go into the kitchen, and you can sort of whisper that it would be, quote, 'bad' if word got out around the office for me, that is why it only happened that one time far, far away."

"Oh babe. You are so good. That is great.

Then what?" He looked at me anxiously.

"Then you just follow along. I will be back in the room by then, and I'm sure you will be able to tell where I take the conversation. Don't be pushy though. This is definitely a delicate conversation on two sides, work, and the gay thing."

"Right, right. No worries."

I swooshed him out with a wave of my hands. "Leave the door open so I can hear." I said in a theatrical whisper.

He nodded, and made sure to leave the door open a good four inches.

He went straight for the kitchen, and started his apology as instructed. "Hey man. Sorry about that, you know. I haven't seen her in a month and…"

Jeremy chimed in with some manly laughter. "Perfectly understandable. If she weren't my boss, I would have to try and hit on her. No offense."

I heard him pop two beer tops as he said, "None taken. She is one hot piece of ass. You kept asking me about what happened in Japan, and I was getting so worked up, I had to go play with her."

"Right on." Jeremy encouraged with words, more manly laughter, and what must have been a high-five from the slap of skin I heard. "So you guys really did it? With another girl I mean?"

"Yup. Haven't you? You are a young studly guy. We all want it, I know. I guess not every man is as lucky as I am, to have a woman who will go with it."

"Oh, yea. I've had a few three-somes. I guess I am pretty lucky that way."

Matthew got excited at this news, "No way! A few!? Where do you find all these people who are open to that kind of stuff?"

"I go to this club. It's nothing but people who want to fuck other people's spouses, swapping, orgies, the whole nine yards." He said casually.

"Oh man! You are going to have to tell me where it is, so I can see if she will go there. That sounds awesome. So wait." His excitement tempered and his voice took on a serious, probing tone as he asked the next question. "Both sides are having three-somes? Like a two men and one woman thing?"

"Yea, sure. It's all about sex, nothing more. Just bodies enjoying pleasure. A lot of them are married couples just looking to spice up the bedroom after the honeymoon wears off. Then they realize that it's something they like to do all the time. Occasionally, people will actually turn into what they call Poly-relationships."

"What's that?" Matthew asked. I could hear him truly getting interested in what Jeremy was saying.

Jeremy continued, "A poly is three or more

people who live like they are all married. I don't know, everyone is different. Some people will swap completely, some only want one other person at a time."

"Wow. I never knew things like that were happening right here in my neighborhood. So you? Have you had a … you know…a threesome with one woman and another guy?"

"Yea, sure. I'm a single guy. That is how it usually is with single guys."

I decided this was far enough into the conversation, that I should come in now. The light was on completely, no questions asked. Matthew knew that Jeremy would go there.

I heard Matthew give Jeremy a slight shush and says, "Not sure we can go there though, you know. Her being the boss and everything."

I popped my beer on the way over to the couch and said, "What are you two whispering about?"

Jeremy cleared his throat. "Well, I believe your husband wants me to agree to silence, that what goes on here in your house today, is never to be spoken of outside of here. Which of course, I would agree to wholeheartedly." He smiled at Matthew, and sat back to drink his beer.

I looked at Matthew and said with a smile, "And what pray tell would Jeremy need to keep so secret?"

"Ah…babe. Well, I might have let slip about

something that happened in Japan. And ah… remember how you said you wanted to look at the option of doing it again." He said it all perfectly, as if I didn't know a thing about what was going on.

I put my hands to my cheeks to cover a mock blushing, "Oh my god. I am so embarrassed. Jeremy, please, please, don't tell anyone about this. I am so sorry he led you down this path."

Jeremy sat up with a concerned look on his face. "No, you don't have to worry about anything like that. Matthew made his little…slip as he calls it and that made me relax. I ah…do that all the time. In fact, I was telling Matthew where you guys can go to meet other people who like to do that, here locally if you want."

"Well…it should have been something we talked about. I don't like the idea of talking to someone I work with about this."

Jeremy again added, "Well, actually, I would be interested in doing more than talking to you about it."

Matthew added, "Yea babe, he thinks you are hot. Says he would have hit on you before now if he had known you were into things like this." He opened his legs and gestured toward his crotch for emphasis.

I looked between the two of them, then focused on Matthew. "And you are ok with this?

A man, I mean? You said you wouldn't even consider it, yet here you are instigating…and with one of my guys."

Matthew moved closer to me so he could get his arm around me to gently squeeze my butt a little. "Yes, babe. I wouldn't have been drilling him all these questions to find out if he would or not, if I wasn't ok with it."

Jeremy piped in, "You were drilling me?" He chuckled.

Matthew gestured with is free hand for Jeremy to come over. "Come sit on the other side of Terry. I think we all need to get closer if we want anything to actually happen." To me he said, "You're ok with this? Right babe?" He kissed me, and I felt the couch give way to Jeremy next to me and my pussy flooded in preparation.

My body melted just slightly, Matthew knew I was ready.

To Jeremy he said, "Go ahead man. She's into it. I can tell." He kissed me harder and I felt Jeremy's hand on my arm as he kissed my shoulder.

I let a rush of air escape, and said to Matthew, "Thank you babe. You would be amazed at the dreams I have been having…about another man with us."

My breathing quickened as Jeremy caressed my breast, then slid his hand up my shirt to get contact with skin. My skin tingled at his touch, yearning for more. Matthew saw this, and helped by taking my shirt off. Jeremy responded by going to his knees on the floor and putting his mouth on my nipple. As he suckled my breast I sucked at the air. I turned to Matthew, and he leaned in for a full tongue kiss. We hadn't kissed like that in so long, it sent a new set of chills running down my spine.

Matthew put his hands down my shorts and his fingers found the river that was already flowing.

"Babe, I think you like this." He chided.

I spread my legs so he could have more access. "I have literally been dreaming about this for the last two weeks straight. I am so ready for it," I whispered.

Matthew pushed three fingers in as far as he could go. My head jerked back in pleasure as I moaned.

Jeremy stood up and unzipped his pants. "Can she suck my cock? Do you want to see that?"

Matthew was continuously thrusting his fingers up inside me. He said, "What do you think babe? Would you like to suck his cock? I'd like to see you suck his cock, I think that would be hot."

"Oh yes." I moaned from the fingered pleasure below and the thoughts of how amazing his cock would feel in my mouth. Shivers quaked through me again. "Yes, baby. I want to suck his cock for you. Will that turn you on?"

Matthew kissed me and said, "Babe, you are not going to believe how rock hard I am already. This whole thing is so turning me on."

Just then, Jeremy's beast emerged and both Matthew and I said, "Wow!" We laughed at each other.

"Man, I don't know if I want to show mine now." Matthew said with humor. "I am hung like a stud field mouse compared to that." We all laughed.

I glanced at Matthew's face to see his reaction as I reached my hand toward Jeremy's horse-like appendage. I was pleased to find he was intrigued by it. He had more eyes for Jeremy's cock than my hand. He watched intently as it pulsed with approval, then I grabbed it and slowly started stroking it. The head revealed itself as I pulled the foreskin back. In and out the head went. Jeremy's breathing quickened, he threw his head back at the long awaited pleasure we both had avoided for the past two weeks. As I turned to focus on what I wanted, I heard Matthew's breathing quicken as well.

Matthew said, "Damn baby. I've never really seen an uncircumcised one up close and personal. Are you gonna be able to get that in your mouth?"

He was waiting for me to do it. He wanted to see it. I turned my body toward Jeremy to get a good angle and said, "Well, let's see."

I wrapped my lips around his head as I pulled his foreskin back and he moaned. I sucked just past the head at first. Matthew had lost concentration on my pussy, and was avidly transfixed on me sucking Jeremy's cock. It made me so crazy horny, for some reason, to know Matthew was enjoying it too.

Matthew praised, "Wow babe. Yes. Suck it." His fingers began to push in and out of me again. "Look at that…stretching your mouth like a good girl. Go down deep baby, show him what you got."

I obeyed. I started to push further down his shaft.

Matthew stood up and slid off his sweat pants now. "Damn! Take it babe. Take it further." He encouraged like a good cheerleader. "That is fucking beautiful. My wife, the cock sucking hottie."

I could see him stroking his own cock out of the corner of my eye, so I reached over with my other hand and took over for him.

Jeremy saw this, and said, "You are about to get fucked by two cocks Terry. You are so hot."

I began to reach the furthest depths of my throat. I gagged slightly and pulled back.

"Holy shit babe. That was so fucking hot!" Matthew was beyond excited now. "Hey, stand up a sec so I can get these blasted shorts off you."

I did as ordered, smiling up at Jeremy as he stroked his penis waiting patiently.

Matthew directed me, "Here, go on your knees here on the couch, that way I can fuck you while you suck him."

This was developing nicely. I was about to turn my fantasy into reality. I hopped onto the couch, positioned myself so that Matthew had one leg on the couch. The other on the floor. He spat in his hand and rubbed it quickly on the head of his now fully erect penis. Jeremy maneuvered in front of me. I turned back to him so he could gently slide his cock back in my mouth.

I moaned lightly, and then louder as Matthew penetrated me from behind. He went slow at first, taking a cue from Jeremy's rhythm. When he had worked the entire shaft in and grabbed my hips to push as deep as it would go, I was ready for more.

I loved my husband's cock. It fit my pussy quite well. The gorgeous cock in front of me was filling my mouth. It sent electric shocks throughout my body. We all made our own noises as the pace started to quicken. I was the steady orifice, they began to pound into me deeper and deeper.

My gagging started, Jeremy placed his hands on the back of my head to help me push it further.

With each gagging reaction, my pussy clenched. It made Matthew moan with pleasure.

"Fuck me babe. That feels so fucking good. Are you ok?"

I pulled back long enough to clear my throat and said, "Oh god yes. This is amazing. It's just like I dreamed about."

He smiled, and said to Jeremy, "Well there you go. You got the green light dude. Fuck my wife's face with that beast.

I put my lips around his head again and Jeremy started to speed up his rhythm. Each stroke he pushed a little deeper. I could feel his hands begin to squeeze my head, I knew he was going to fuck my throat hard.

I relaxed my throat as much as I could, maneuvering to elongate the path.

Matthew was thrusting at the same pace. "Oh shit yea. He's fucking your mouth babe. Suck that cock like a good girl. Make her gag again man. Make her pussy clench."

Jeremy shifted his hands slightly. I knew it was about to happen. He was going all the way. I took a deep breath and he plunged his cock as far as it would go. I gagged, my pussy clenched, Matthew moaned. Jeremy made small little pumps, thrusting his head down my throat even further. My throat was stretched, the gagging made a river of juices flood out my pussy over Matthew's cock, and down my legs.

"Holy shit babe. You like that?" He began pounding my pussy so hard and fast, Jeremy didn't need to move anymore. Matthew was pushing me onto Jeremy's cock. I couldn't hold on any longer…my body was wracked with an orgasm, and I was suffocating. Jeremy gave one final push and then pulled out.

I coughed and got control of my throat again. Saliva was dripping uncontrollably from my mouth. Matthew continued his jack-hammer pace for a few, then realized we had taken a pause.

"Oh my fucking god babe that was hot! Your pussy just went crazy. Can you do that again?"

I went back to sucking Jeremy's cock for a few strokes and then asked, "Matthew baby, can I let him fuck me?"

"Shit yea! Can I make you gag like he did? That was so fucking hot." To Jeremy he said, "Go ahead man. My wife has a nice tight little pussy." He giggled a little, "Will be even tighter for you." He watched Jeremy's trophy with admiration as he came over to tag him out.

I sat on the edge of the couch, Jeremy got on his knees between my legs. I motioned to Matthew to get his cock up to my mouth, he jumped up next to me and slid it in.

Jeremy gently touched my pussy with the tip of his penis, he started moving it in small circles. My lips opened as he pushed just a little, until the head popped in. My body reacted with a spasm of pleasure.

Matthew instructed Jeremy, "Yea, do that about 20 times. She loves it when just the head pops in." He watched intently with a smile. Jeremy's cock slowly penetrated me and then came out with my lips pulling at him trying to suck him back inside me.

The teasing is what really sent me over the top. The last two weeks of waiting to have him again added to it. I was clawing at him to fill me. Matthew continued his slow, rhythmic penetration of my mouth so I couldn't say anything other than moaning.

Finally, Jeremy pushed deep. My back arched and a scream of pleasure escaped around my husband's cock. He pounded in, over and over, till eventually, Matthew knew I was about to cum.

My husband pulled his cock free of my mouth to allow me full range of motion, I threw my head back and cried out, "I'm cumming! Oh god, I'm cumming!"

Matthew joined the revelry, "Yea baby, make her cum, make her cum. Keep fucking her hard, don't stop.

My screams of ecstasy continued as Jeremy continued. My body was shaking beyond anything I had ever experienced before.

Finally, it subsided, and Jeremy slowed his pace.

Jeremy said to Matthew, "Thank you man."

"Holy crap man. I've never seen her cum that hard before. You are the champ. Thank you. I just hope that's not all. We aren't finished yet."

"No, not at all. Hey, you guys want to try some DP?" Jeremy asked as he pulled his cock out and stroked it.

Matthew looked at me and said, "Sure, I think we are up for anything, right babe?"

Breathlessly, I said, "If it makes me cum again, I'm up for it."

To Matthew I said, "That was so erotic having your cock in my mouth while he was fucking me. I know it was really great sex with Ashley, but I think this beats it." We all laughed as I stood up.

To Jeremy I inquired, "What is DP?"

Jeremy replied, "Double penetration. You kind of had DP just now, technically. When someone says DP though, they are usually talking about DP in your nether regions. You can do one in the ass and one in the pussy, or both in one."

"Wow!" I said. "I'm not sure I can put both of you in one. You are already more than I have ever had before, Jeremy."

Matthew was bouncing up and down, "it's all good babe, we can start with one in each hole. I love that idea." He looked confused, "How do we set it up Jer?"

Jeremy took over with instructions, "Matthew, you sit on the couch now. Terry, sit on his lap facing me. You guys get him in your ass."

I held up my hands, "Wait a minute. I can't just do ass fucking at the drop of a dime like a porn star. I have to get worked up to that."

Matthew said, "Yea, yea, yea, I know babe. You come straddle me, we will get you worked up and in, then you can switch around."

How could these guys do this so smoothly? Even though I knew this was the first time Matthew had ever done something like this before, it was like they had rehearsed it. I straddled my husband, slamming my pussy down around him. Full, deep penetration. Then I began to rub my clit up and down. I leaned into him and we kissed passionate kisses. It was the first time in years that I had truly felt his desire for me.

He spread my butt cheeks and Jeremy bent down to lick my asshole. I felt the muscles loosen. I arched my back so he had more access, and he got down on his knees to continue his business. Matthew spread his legs to give him more room.

"Matthew," Jeremy said. "I'm going to be licking her asshole, taint, and her pussy."

"Yea man, no problem. Go to it." Matthew said distractedly.

"Well, I just wanted to let you know, because you are probably going to feel my tongue on your cock occasionally, and I didn't want you to freak out or anything."

I stopped moving for a moment, curious to

see where this would lead.

Matthew easily replied, "Yea, no worries. I heard you earlier. This is all just pleasure and sex right? You're not gonna be my boyfriend or anything weird right?"

"Right. It's all just pleasure, enjoy it." I said, and began grinding again while Jeremy went down.

I could feel his tongue everywhere. He made sweeping motions across my taint and around my asshole. I opened to him and he plunged his thick tongue up next to Matthew's cock.

Matthew moaned and whispered, "Oh fuck. That feels good."

I pushed my weight down onto Matthew's cock, deeper, while getting Jeremy's tongue deeper into my ass at the same time.

Jeremy's tongue continued, he massaged the flat against my taint, just like I was massaging my clit on Matthew's stomach.

Matthew whispered to me, "Oh baby. That feels so fucking good. His tongue is licking my shaft."

My head fell back with an explosion of excitement. "Yes! Oh yes. Babe, stick it in my ass. I'm so ready for it."

Before Matthew could respond, Jeremy thrust his tongue in my ass and I screamed with a new kind of orgasm. He used his thumb next, the rest of his fingers going down around my pussy, and tightening on Matthew as I continued to rock my pelvis through the next orgasm.

I pulled forward slightly so Matthew's cock could come out to go in my asshole. Jeremy grabbed it and guided it.

I could feel Matthew tense up slightly as another man took hold of his penis. Then I positioned my ass so he could enter easily. Jeremy began stroking Matthew's cock. My ass slowly loosened with each stroke, allowing Matthew to penetrate further and further.

Matthew moaned. "Oh! Oh yes. That's it babe. That fucking ass is so sweet. God! This feels so fucking good."

Jeremy's hand had released Matthew. I was slamming down on him repeatedly. Jeremy stood back and watched, stroking his long beautiful cock. I wanted him inside me again.

I stopped the action and pulled off of my husband.

Matthew protested, "What what?"

Then he understood as I turned around, sliding myself back down, over his erection. This time facing away from him, carefully positioning, then slowly lowering myself onto his cock, allowing him to penetrate my yearning asshole.

He said, "Oh yes. Oh that's a good, little, naughty girl." He sucked air in as I stroked him with my tightness a few times, then laid back on him and spread my legs in the air.

Jeremy smiled as he saw his invitation,

coming to me at once.

He was about to dive in when I put my hand on his chest to stop him. I sat back up and continued a slow grind on my husband. I took Jeremy in my mouth again, his fullness stretched my jaw. He took my head and pushed harder than he ever had before. He knew this would drive me crazy, his pushing became the gas pedal for our tournament. The speed at which I sucked his cock caused my husband to increase the speed at which he fucked my ass. My pussy was throbbing for more.

Jeremy had both hands on my head again. His body began to tense, he was about to cum. I pushed my head further and gagged hard. Matthew moaned with the pleasurable reaction he received from his end. I pulled my mouth away, to prevent the crescendo before its time, and laid back on Matthew again.

This time, when I spread my legs, Jeremy quickly positioned himself, thrusting his cock into my pussy. It slid easily in, with my saliva to grease the way. It was a sensation I had never felt before. I felt engorged, pleasantly, and the pressure was so intense, it was on the brink of pain…I was in ecstasy.

Jeremy slowly fucked his cock in and out, making his way deeper and deeper. Matthew began a slow undulation as well. I could feel both of them inside me. Matthew moaned in pleasure, he felt a new sensation as well.

He whispered behind me, "I can feel him inside you… just on the other side."

Rhythmically, we made music with our moans, the smacking and slurping of my orifices as they clamored for more. The juices of our pleasured outpourings obediently flowed to ensure maximum enjoyment. My mind slipped into another realm as my body tingled and was fulfilled.

Jeremy found my mouth with his tongue and plunged it deep. I fantasized about a third guy joining us, filling my mouth while they filled me below. An orgy came into focus in my mind. My body craved more.

Jeremy must have sensed my yearning. He put three of his fingers in my mouth along side his tongue. New shivers of excitement surged through my body. Matthew watched in amazement. He exhaled heavily to show his pleasure.

Jeremy momentarily removed his tongue and looked to Matthew, "Support her head and push as I thrust my fingers in. I think she likes to be gagged. You guys have a dildo?"

"Oh yeah." Matthew did as instructed, I could feel his engorgement throb with his pleasure. Under me, he rotated his hips more so each thrust seemed further and deeper. "Yes, we have one. I'm not sure I want to get up at the moment to get it." He groaned as his cock hit in and

Jeremy sped up.

"No. Not yet." Jeremy said breathlessly. His arms tensed up, he began slamming me with his pelvis as he drove himself deeper as well.

He repositioned slightly so he could grab my hips, the movement became double-time. With each slap of skin, fireworks exploded within my body. Each explosion of endorphins rendered me paralyzed. Jeremy continued for an incredible amount of time at this breakneck speed until finally, he screamed out. As his orgasm escaped him, his hips slammed into me like a sledge hammer breaking concrete, for a slower final fulmination.

I cried out with each crescendo, "AH! YES!"

I could feel Matthew beneath me quivering, his back arched momentarily as he thrust a final blast as well.

We were all breathless and spent. My body felt like glitter rained down with the occasional after-shock. No one said anything, just breathing could be heard. A peacefulness overtook me. It was tranquil, like wind blowing in the trees on a warm day, when lying in the grass. I could not imagine being able to surpass this experience.

Slowly, Jeremy removed himself from me. I was like a rag-doll, I could do nothing to help or hinder at that moment. I could feel Matthew wanting to escape as well.

"You're going to have to help me get off you

babe. My body is limp with pleasure. That was fucking amazing."

Both of them chuckled agreement. Matthew rolled slightly to the left, helping me slide off his softening erection. Our three sweat glistened bodies laid on the couch, one next to the other.

Finally, Matthew recovered his breath, he was the first to speak. "Holy Shit Batman! That was like… I don't even know what… Out of this world!"

Jeremy took a deep, regulating breath and simply smiled. It was like he knew he had just given us the crème de la crème, and he was proud of it.

Time crept on and a quiet set in. The music had finished somewhere in the middle of our expedition. My thoughts were everywhere. What's next? Will we do it some more? Now? Ever? I want Jeremy to stay, but I know Matthew will find it awkward.

Jeremy stood and headed to the bathroom, grabbing his clothes on the way.

Matthew reached over and lazily patted my leg. "Wow babe! You really know how to bring home presents. I never would'a thought this would be my thing, but damn, that was good." He smiled. Already reminiscing about the event. "I guess we can switch back and forth, a girl one time, then a guy. Huh?"

"Yes, sure babe."

I decided it was time to get moving. Jeremy was dressing so he could leave, and I should have been playing the good hostess. I needed to get my butt dressed at least in some fashion. Having Matthew dreaming of all these other people we would be doing was not sitting well with me. Once again, it seemed to me that his only concern was having other people to fuck.

I grabbed a towel from our hamper in the bedroom, and did a quick cleanup of the cocktail between my legs. I grabbed my silk bathrobe, putting it on as I exited our bedroom. Jeremy was just coming out of the bathroom.

He bent down and kissed me hard yet brief. I wanted more from him. I wanted to be alone with him but I knew that was not going to happen. What is it about him? Why is he any different than Matthew?

Matthew had come around the corner and Jeremy reached his hand out for a shake. "Man, that was great. I'm gonna leave the two of you alone now to relax."

Matthew vigorously shook back and with a huge grin said, "You're tellin' me. That was great. We need to do it again some time."

As the words escaped him, I could sense somehow that it would not happen again. No matter how much we had all enjoyed it, there were unspoken words and emotions swarming around us to prevent it. Hornets that could strike at any moment and cause us all to flee in different directions.

The boys politely and properly said their goodbyes. Jeremy pecked me impersonally on the cheek. The door closed on that chapter in my life.

Epilogue

I often thought about it all. It was like a first kiss. The way your body felt when you'd been flirting with someone, had a first date, and then finally, you kiss. Like the first time I had kissed Matthew. Like the first time I kissed Ashley and Jeremy. The latter were more exhilarating, as I recalled, due to them having been forbidden. The three-some with Jeremy was like that too. It had that first kiss feeling about it, never to be achieved again.

Matthew tried. We began visiting the swinger places. We even brought home a couple of different men at different times, but I never felt anything remotely as exotic as when we had Jeremy.

Ashley was a great first too. I believed I had more of a connection with her when it was just the two of us. When we added Matthew to the mix, well… it didn't mix well. We looked for women to bring home. We found that a woman was much more difficult to obtain, though we did manage it once.

We experimented with swapping couples. Matthew thought that was great of course. It didn't really matter what the situation was, for him, it meant he got to fuck another woman. I didn't really get into that aspect of it. I didn't know these men that I lay with. We had no connection other than an assumed desire to have sex with anyone and everyone.

Most of the time the men weren't half as attractive as the women. If the woman wasn't attractive we wouldn't go after them because Matthew couldn't get it up. Yet time and time again, I would be stuck doing some older rich fart, with a hot young wife. Wee fun... Not.

Never did I feel the first kiss experience again, at least not with Matthew.

About the Author

Hi, I am Samantha Writner. I grew up in the cold north of Philadelphia. As a child I swore to never live there when I got older. I have kept to my word and now roam the southern states, the islands, and even further south countries. I don't actually have a permanent home base, and with my love for travel, it suits me fine.

My favorite saying is, "Pretend to be an Extrovert, it keeps the blues away." Using this way of thinking has afforded me to meet many friends and hear many stories.

I hope you have enjoyed *Threesomes Cum*. It is book 1 of 3. The next in the series is *Orgies Cum Together,* and is due out late 2015. Book 3, *Submissives Cum on Command* will be out in 2016.

I would love to hear about your experience and what your thoughts are on the imagery I added. You can leave a comment and chat with me on my publisher's website at:

http://BlackWidowPublishing.com

Connect with Samantha

Like - Follow - Friend
Find Samantha at all of these locations:

Samantha's Publisher:
http://BlackWidowPublishing.com

Samantha's Facebook Page:
https://www.facebook.com/SamanthaWritner

Samantha's Twitter:
https://twitter.com/BlackWidowPress

Bonus

Please enjoy Chapter 1, from Book 2, of the First Kiss Series.

Orgies Cum Together

Swingers are all very different. Some do, some don't, some are picky, and some do anything. Or should I say anyone… But the elusive unicorn is what they all seem to be after. Single women are called unicorns… because they are like mythically creatures in the fact that they are difficult to find.

Don't get me wrong. There are single women around… occasionally. They come and go. They don't seem to stay single long. As with women who are not in the lifestyle, most of them desire to have full-time companionship eventually. Being that they hold the key to sex, they are the ones who determine when and where a relationship begins and ends.

My husband and I had been playing, what I would call 'lightly' in the 'lifestyle' for about a year before I finally told him I wanted a divorce. It's not a common thing to hear about swingers getting divorced actually. Usually, they are determined to stay together. It's one reason couples get into the lifestyle to begin with. Some are very secure couples that are committed to their marriage and perhaps need, or just want, a little spice added to their sex life. Others though, they may have the end in sight and truly want to avoid it, so they begin exploring options that may solve the issue. I actually knew I was leaving him before we went to our first swinger event.

We were not really well matched from the very get go. It was my fault for hooking up with him in the first place. I was an over the top braniac, and he was funny. I wanted amusement in my life, and he supplied it, for a time. You would think with all my intelligence, I would have thought better of such a poor match.

We had been struggling in the bedroom when we had our first threesome with Ashley a few years back. It was amazing. I fell in love with her. It made my sex life with Matthew crazy good for a while. Problem was, I had to fantasize about Ashley to get aroused.

Then there was Jeremy. He brought me to the other side of threesomes. He made me question myself, and wonder at how I had arranged my life. My connection with him ran deep. Too deep actually. I broke my vows of marriage with him. Not that I hadn't technically already done that with Ashley. It just felt different, as it was with another man this time.

At that point, I already knew the marriage was doomed. So I brought Jeremy home with me… to Matthew. I wasn't sure how he would react to me bringing home a man. With a bit of tactful communication both from me, and from Jeremy, we got him steered to the path we wanted him on.

It sounds like I was cruel. I can assure you, Matthew thought it was an amazing night. I still have not met its' match. I was in the thralls of ecstasy, yet wanting even more. My first thoughts of a full scale orgy happened that night.

Matthew and I had a few nights of great follow up sex after Jeremy. Then it quickly waned again. It was only two weeks later, on Thursday evening when I arrived home from work, he came bounding up to me like a kid again.

"Hey babe!" He gave me a quick peck on the cheek, which was our version of romance these days now. "Guess what I found?"

It was like tripping around a young puppy overly excited to greet his owner, as I was trying to get in the door and put my things down. I gracefully danced past him so I could shut the door and get my coat off. "Yes dear. What did you find?" I failed at keeping the disdainful tone out of my voice.

"I was looking online, like Jeremy suggested, and found a swinger club!"

The excitement in his facial expression irritated me to no end. How did he never seem to get the fact that it pissed me off that all he ever wanted was to have sex with other people? "That's great dear."

"Well, I was thinking we could go there tomorrow night. You know…check it out." He waited for my answer.

I pulled a beer out of the fridge, popped the top, and took a drink before answering. "Sure babe, that would be fun. I'm sure he will be looking for a woman most likely. I'll check out the guys, at least enjoy this in some way.

"Awesome! I will post that we are going." He turned to head to the computer.

"Who are you posting to?"

"Oh, I created an account for us on this website. We can look at, and chat with other swingers. People post if they are going so we can check each other out I guess." He disappeared into the office.

So we are officially swingers? I walked into the bedroom to get out of my work clothes.

I grabbed my sweat-pants and a t-shirt, closing the bathroom door behind me. I don't even want him looking at me anymore. How am I going to hang out with him and be social with people he wants to fuck? I have to end this.

Dialing the water to my favorite temperature I finished my beer. After closing the drain and re-testing the temperature of the water I headed back to the kitchen to grab two more. That should be enough to last through my bath. Most women preferred bubbles for relaxation, I liked my bubbles in a bottle. It's the only way I can deal with him.

He was still sitting at the computer as I passed by. I could see pictures of mostly naked people, dick and pussy close-ups even. Rolling my eyes, I pop another top and restrain myself from slamming the bathroom door.

I shrugged back out of my comfy clothes as I whispered my rehearsal, "Matthew, I'm leaving you. … What? You can't leave, I haven't had enough sex with other people yet. … That is exactly why I am leaving you, you just don't get it. I don't want to have sex with *you* any more. It repulses me that you want to be a swinger. … But I thought you liked it too. … I do like having multiple people, I just don't want any of them to be you."

The heat on my feet as I climbed into the tub ceases my thoughts for only a brief second. God, I love a good hot bath…by myself. I can't wait to be able to come home to an empty house. I need to tell him soon. Fuck! Why was I so stupid to marry him?

The more I drank, my thoughts drifted to memories. Soft pale skin, freckles. Scent of vanilla that she loved to wear. The taste of her pussy in my mouth, like a Georgia peach. Soft fuzz tickling my lip, juices running down my chin. Plunging my tongue into the sweetness.

My fingers played with my clit as the memories filled it with arousal. … I'm being fucked from behind…by Jeremy. His cock slams inside me over and over. I want it in my mouth. I love his cock in my mouth.

My fingers press down outside my labia. The vision of his cock, the memory of feeling it in my mouth, stretching my jaw. Two fingers in my pussy. Even in the water it is slick with excitement.

Her tongue circling, tingles run though my body. She grabs my hips as my body bucks with an impending orgasm, and her thick tongue dives in, heightening the pleasure further. Yes. Make me cum.

KNOCK KNOCK KNOCK

I jumped, knocking my beer into the tub. "Shit! What?"

"Hey…um…just wanted to know if you wanted to have sex?"

My breathing was quick, I was so close to cumming. If you had given me just twenty more seconds…

Softer, he clarified, "I was looking at all the pictures of the people we might be meeting, and ah… I kinda got a hard on."

My eyes roll again. I dare not answer as he will hear my irritability.

"Babe? You ok in there?"

Finally I say, "Yeah, sure. Give me a sec. I'll be right there." Fuck me. Why did I say yes? Because you don't want to hurt him… you would like to have a big cock pounding your pussy right now… you don't want to have to tell him you are leaving him right this second…

I grab my towel and do a quick dry off as I step out. Opening the door I look back at my hot bath. It might still be warm enough when I get back.

Turning to look at him laying on the bed, stroking his erection. I focus on the object of my desire, I don't need to look at him. Just fuck him, get off and be done.

He smiled as he looks at my wet body. If it involves sex, he is all about me. At least when it's just the two of us.

I didn't bother with getting him wet, my pussy is plenty lubed up. I straddled him on the bed. He pointed it straight up and I lowered myself onto him. "Mmmm."

"Oh. Yea." His eyes closed with the pleasure of the first plunge.

I have to admit to myself, it feels so good. He fills me. I slowly start rocking my hips, rubbing my clit on him.

"That's it baby. Fuck my cock good. I can't wait to see another cock fucking your pussy again, feel it inside with me." He grabs my hips, forcing me to move faster. "Yea, that's it."

I close my eyes envisioning Jeremy stuffing my mouth. I see him holding my head, pushing the head down my throat. Fuck my mouth. Yes!

My pussy releases another flood of juices. I see him coming down in front of me. I am sitting on Matthew's lap, his cock deep in my pussy. Jeremy is going to stick his in too. How it had stretched my pussy deliciously as both of them entered me. "Oh yea. Fuck my pussy baby. Matthew, I want you to fuck me from behind."

I stopped and climbed off him.

He jumped to obey. Positioning behind me, he slides in and then pounds me like a jack hammer. I think of my first night with Jeremy. He had fucked me for hours. He fucked me from behind, grabbing my tits. I see him fucking me like this again, using Matthew's motions to add the trueness of feeling. My hips rock. I am like a dog in the throws, unable to control my body.

"Yes! Fuck! Oh yea, Oh yea, that's it, that's it, yes."

"Yea baby. I'm gonna slam that pussy till you explode."

"Yes! Fuck me! Fuck me! That's it, that's it." My body reacts to the cock inside me. Spasms of pleasure begin. "I'm gonna cum baby. That's it! Fuck me harder!" He digs, in and slams me harder and faster.

"Oh baby, that's it. Cum on my cock. Yes, that's it. Squirt those juices all over me." His rhythm becomes erratic. He grits his teeth as he growls, "Fuck baby, you're gonna make me cum."

I feel his dick expand. Our skin grinds, the friction is good. The final strokes are so hard my body explodes again. He grunts, and then holds my hips to him. He growls deeply as he releases. I feel his cock spasm with his ejaculation. It taps on my G-spot, and sends more sparkles rippling though my body.

It's very short, although very satisfying. We do know how to do it for each other.

He pulls out, and we both collapse on the bed to catch our breath. As my breathing regulates I feel sleep overtaking me.

More to cum...

Get a $1 coupon for Book 2
Visit:
http://blackwidowpublishing.com/
black-widow-readers-club/

Sign up for the Reader's Club and get
publisher's discounts on all the books made at
Black Widow Publishing.